Growing Up Ivy

Growing Up Ivy

Peggy Dymond Leavey

Growing Up Ivy

a novel

DUNDURN PRESS

TORONTO

Editor: Allison Hirst
Design: Jennifer Scott
Printer: Webcom

Library and Archives Canada Cataloguing in Publication

Leavey, Peggy Dymond
    Growing up Ivy : a novel / by Peggy Dymond Leavey.

ISBN 978-1-55488-723-1

    I. Title.

PS8573.E2358G76 2010   jC813'.54   C2009-907480-X

1   2   3   4   5   14   13   12   11   10

Conseil des Arts du Canada   Canada Council for the Arts   Canadä   ONTARIO ARTS COUNCIL / CONSEIL DES ARTS DE L'ONTARIO

We acknowledge the support of the **Canada Council for the Arts** and the **Ontario Arts Council** for our publishing program. We also acknowledge the financial support of the **Government of Canada** through the **Canada Book Fund** and **The Association for the Export of Canadian Books**, and the **Government of Ontario** through the **Ontario Book Publishers Tax Credit program**, and the **Ontario Media Development Corporation**.

Care has been taken to trace the ownership of copyright material used in this book. The author and the publisher welcome any information enabling them to rectify any references or credits in subsequent editions.

J. Kirk Howard, President

Printed and bound in Canada.
www.dundurn.com

Dundurn Press
3 Church Street, Suite 500
Toronto, Ontario, Canada
M5E 1M2

Gazelle Book Services Limited
White Cross Mills
High Town, Lancaster, England
LA1 4XS

Dundurn Press
2250 Military Road
Tonawanda, NY
U.S.A. 14150

Mixed Sources
Product group from well-managed forests, controlled sources and recycled wood or fiber
www.fsc.org Cert no. SW-COC-002358
© 1996 Forest Stewardship Council
FSC

98%

ANCIENT FOREST ™ FRIENDLY

To the real Miss Derek,
the teacher who started it all

Acknowledgements

I would like to acknowledge the assistance of the County of Prince Edward Public Library, the Quinte West Public Library, and the Toronto Reference Library in directing me to sources relating to the Great Depression; also Robert Paul, editor/publisher of the online typewriter museum, for finding the Corona 3.

Special thanks to my mother-in-law, Janet Brinklow Leavey, for telling me what it was like for a young girl growing up in the Dirty Thirties, and to the original members of my writing group, Women of Words, for their support and encouragement, and for believing in Ivy.

Prologue

Ivy woke to the sound of whispering. She lay perfectly still, eyes wide, her ears straining.

The moon shone in through the window at the back of the caravan. Something rustled away through the dry grass underneath.

"Ivy." The whispered voice came again.

"Momma?" Ivy said, out loud.

"Don't try to find me, darling girl."

In the moonlight, Ivy saw Alva roll over onto his other side. "You're dreaming again, Ivy," he said.

Prologue

PART ONE

Ivy

1
Leaving Mrs. Bingley's

On an early June morning in 1931, a tall child, dark hair in two long braids, elbowed open the door of a Toronto diner. She was wearing a shapeless blue coat, in spite of the warm weather, and carrying a suitcase in her arms, as if it had no handle.

She set the suitcase into the nearest booth and, slipping off the coat, sat down facing the door.

Her mother had just deserted her — up and left the day before — and the girl, whose name was Ivy, not yet thirteen. At least, that's the story her grandmother would always tell. Ivy didn't happen to see it that way.

Gloria Klein, a waitress at the diner, hurried over to take her order. When she saw that her customer was young Ivy Chalmers, she stuck her pencil into her hairnet and took a seat beside the suitcase.

"She did it, didn't she?" Gloria said, a grim look on her freckled face. "Frannie's taken off."

"Taken off?" Ivy shrugged. "She's gone to New York, like she said she would. And she wants to be called *Frances* now, Gloria. Now that she's going to be a star."

Gloria blew out a loud breath. "Well, she'll always be just Frannie to me. We've been friends too long for anything else. Anyway, I'm *glad* she got away from this dump."

Ivy cast a puzzled look around at the diner's shiny surfaces, causing Gloria to add, "I meant the neighbourhood, Ivy. But let's face it; Frannie's whole life was a dump. Except you, of course, sweet cakes."

She reached across and grabbed Ivy's hands. "Oh, my golly, Frannie'd kill me if I ever made you think you weren't the best thing that ever happened to her."

❧

Yesterday, when Ivy came home from school and found the old cardboard suitcase packed with all her things and her mother's few possessions gone from their room at Mrs. Bingley's, she knew where her mother had gone, and why. For weeks Frannie had been telling her that if things worked out the way she hoped, she'd be leaving Toronto for New York City.

14

Frances Chalmers was an actress. Her most recent role was the lead in a production that had just closed at the Rivoli. Everyone who'd seen the play said Frances showed great potential. Especially the director, who had promised to take her to Broadway and make her famous.

"You're going to remember 1931, Frannie baby," the director told her. "This is the year you become a star."

Along with the suitcase, Frannie had left a note for Ivy on the table.

Ivy, dearest

The rent on Shangri-La is paid for to-night but in the morning you must go to Gloria at the diner. She will take you to your grandmother. Wait there for me.

Let's pretend that your grandmother is the dowager <u>Queen of Siam</u>. You will have a glorious time with her because as a granddaughter you will be the princess of the kingdom.

Another new world, Ivy! Fresh adventures for you to imagine.

Darling girl, you must write and tell me all the wonderful things you are do-

*ing in Siam. I will send you my address
the minute I am settled in New York.*

*Your loving,
Momma*

Tucked under the chipped edge of a saucer that held two sugared doughnuts was a letter addressed to Ivy's grandmother. Ivy had never met the person whose name was on the envelope. Maud Chalmers had to be Papa's mother. And in that case, Maud's home in Larkin, Ontario, could very well be where he would finally come to find her.

Ivy slept under her coat that night because the blanket had disappeared from the bed. The landlady must have seen Frannie leave the house with all her bundles and come upstairs immediately to collect whatever she'd left behind.

Although her mother was often gone until well past midnight, Ivy couldn't remember ever having to spend an entire night alone. The scrabbling of mice between the walls kept her awake. She wished she hadn't eaten both of the doughnuts before she'd lain down, but she'd been afraid there would be nothing left in the morning.

When sleep wouldn't come, Ivy tried to recall some of the stories she and her mother had shared after they got into bed at night, on those evenings that Frannie was home. She pretended that she was Dorothy, falling asleep in a field of red poppies, on her way to the Emerald City in the Land of Oz.

Ivy opened the door to the hall the next morning. Somewhere in Mrs. Bingley's house someone was cooking breakfast. Even the aroma of burnt toast made Ivy's stomach roll with hunger. She hoped Gloria would find something for her to eat this morning, before they set out together for her grandmother's and the fresh adventures Frannie had promised.

Seeing that the bathroom down the hall was vacant, Ivy scurried in. Mr. Butcher had forgotten his tooth powder on the back of the sink, and she helped herself to some. It tasted much better than the salt she ordinarily used.

After brushing her hair, Ivy carefully braided it, knowing the part at the back was not as straight as it would have been had Frannie been there to help.

She waited until she could no longer hear the sound of children rattling along the street out front, shouting to each other as they made their way to school. Shrugging on her coat to save carrying it, she tucked the letter for her grandmother into the pocket, and with her arms wrapped around the suitcase, went down the stairs to say goodbye to Mrs. Bingley.

2

Life with Frannie

Of all the stories Frannie told, Ivy's favourite was the one about the day she'd been born.

In those days, Frannie worked as a housemaid for Mrs. Hubert Hinkman. "The best job in the world," was the way Frannie described it. "Mrs. Hinkman wasn't just a rich widow lady, Ivy. She was an absolute angel."

On the morning of August 13, 1918, while Frannie was on hands and knees wiping the floor inside the front door of the Hinkman house, Ivy surprised everyone by arriving on the scene, three weeks ahead of schedule.

It was Mrs. Hinkman who found Frannie there on the floor of the foyer, beside the overturned umbrella stand. The grand lady herself brought Ivy into the world, and when it was over, summoned her own doctor to the house.

In the months that followed, the baby spent her days like a perfect little turtle dove, cooing happily from the nest of blankets in an open bureau drawer. Frannie returned to washing the floors and polishing the silver.

Frannie always spoke of the baby's arrival as if Ivy had come into her life as the happiest of accidents. Ivy never inquired where her father was. Not until she started school and learned that most other children seemed to have them.

"Why don't we pretend that your Papa is like the Prince in *Sleeping Beauty*," Frannie said. "One day he will come riding back into your life."

For a long time Ivy was satisfied with that explanation. Every time she heard the clop, clop of a horse's hooves in the street, she would hurry to the window, just in case it was Papa, coming at last. But the woolly horse that pulled the milkman's wagon or the sway-backed mare belonging to the iceman was not the sleek, white charger she pictured her father riding in on.

It was Frannie's job at Mrs. Hinkman's that had sown the seeds to her dream of becoming an actress. Mrs. Hinkman had been a promoter of dramatic and musical productions in the city, keeping the cream of Toronto society entertained throughout the years of the war. According to Frannie, there was an endless stream of interesting people coming and going through the foyer of the Hinkman house.

Once, Mrs. H. had arranged to bring to the city a director from New York by the name of Anna Dunkle. The occasion was a charity benefit, featuring local talent performing skits and choruses.

Miss Dunkle would be staying with Mrs. Hinkman, and when the lady arrived in a chauffeur-driven motor car, Frannie told Ivy that she'd thought the procession of trunks would never stop coming through the door.

"What did you see, Momma?" Ivy begged. "What was in all those trunks?" She never doubted for a moment that the show's promoter and the New York City director would put on a fashion show for the girl who washed the windows.

"Silk scarves of every colour and delicate fans, Ivy," Frannie said. "Long feather boas and necklaces and tiaras, tunics and broadswords — every costume you could imagine." And the two of them would preen and prance about the room as if they themselves were in front of an adoring audience.

Sometime before Ivy's earliest memories began, Mrs. Hinkman died, and Frannie lost her position. Ivy was not yet three. Frannie sold her pretty furniture, and they moved into the flat with her oldest and dearest friend, Gloria Klein. Frannie got a job washing dishes at the hotel where Gloria worked. According to Frannie, Gloria Klein was another absolute angel.

But when Gloria decided to include her boyfriend, Eugene, in the happy household, Frannie and Ivy found a room of their own, across town.

With her arms deep in dishwater, Frannie set in motion her plan to become an actress. The manager of the hotel was kind enough to give her the day-old newspapers that had been left in the lobby, and she and Ivy would scour them every evening, looking for notices of upcoming auditions.

To the armload of fairy stories they brought home from the library, Frannie now added books of plays by Shakespeare and Ibsen, a new volume every week. Ivy would fall asleep listening to her mother's voice, reading all the parts.

It was hard for her mother to keep a job and travel all over the city, trying out for parts in new productions. Frannie lost the dishwashing job at the hotel and began a series of short-term jobs, while she and Ivy moved from one rooming house to another, often just ahead of the bailiff.

If there was no money for the streetcar, Frannie would walk to her audition, sometimes leaving before daybreak. "I'll be leaving early tomorrow morning,

Ivy," she would say. "After you're up and washed, put on your play dress and go down to Mrs. Foster's. She said you could play with Margaret till I get back."

Margaret Foster was a dull girl with a surprising lack of original ideas. With her pale eyes in her pudding face, Margaret would stare blankly at Ivy, and Ivy knew the girl couldn't possibly understand the imaginary places she was trying to evoke.

When Margaret came to find her, Ivy told her, from the other side of the door, that she had developed a mysterious rash and could not play with her today.

"Let me see it," Margaret said.

"Oh, no," Ivy said. "It's very contagious."

Hearing Margaret clump back downstairs, Ivy climbed up onto the bed and played happily with her paper dolls while she waited for Frannie. She knew that no matter how late it became, Frannie would always come home. Ivy had buried her early fears of abandonment somewhere deep inside.

Frannie burst into the room, her blonde curls bouncing. "Good luck today, darling girl."

"Momma! You got the part!"

"No, dear heart, but I got a job scouring pans at the bakery in the next block. I saw their sign in the window just now as I came along. Isn't that wonderful luck? And look what they gave me for our supper."

It was a round cake, jam-filled, its golden-brown top sprinkled with sugar in the shape of a snowflake. Ivy ate so much of it that her stomach ached all night.

That was the year Ivy started school. She could already read, having learned by watching the words as Frannie read to her each night.

The classroom seemed hardly big enough for Ivy and her imagination, and she was often scolded for daydreaming. She much preferred to stay at home, and on those days when she did, she began to write stories of her own, using the back pages of her scribbler. No one from the school ever came looking for her.

❧❧

This morning, when Ivy reached the foot of the stairs, she could hear a radio playing inside Mrs. Bingley's apartment. With a background of organ music, a chorus was singing the praises of some soap that promised a beautiful complexion.

When the deep voice of the announcer intoned, "And now, let us return to our story," Ivy knew the landlady would not be answering the door. She didn't blame her. If she owned a radio she would listen to serials all day long, too.

Frannie used to call Mrs. Bingley "Lady Natalie of Bing," saying that made it easier to forgive her constant criticism.

"Some people think they must comment on the way the rest of us live our lives," Frannie had said, as she hustled Ivy back up the stairs one evening.

Ivy had come down because she'd heard a noisy confrontation between the two women taking place outside Mrs. Bingley's door. Obviously, Lady Natalie had been lying in wait for Frannie's return.

"Of course Ivy's not alone!" Frannie was saying, two bright red spots colouring her porcelain cheeks. "She's never alone. How could she be? There are fourteen other people living in this house."

There were much worse places to live than Mrs. B.'s — like the drafty, two-roomed flat over Klemper's Dry Goods Store. The Klempers had turned out to be impatient landlords who refused to wait even one extra week for their rent.

Frannie was still working at the bakeshop when she and Ivy came home late one afternoon to find all their worldly possessions out on the sidewalk in front of Klemper's store. It had happened before, in other places, and Ivy always wished she could be as brave about it as her mother.

While they stood there in the grey light, surveying

their bundles, it had started to drizzle. "Where will we go now, Momma?" Ivy asked.

"Wherever you wish, my darling. Will we go to Never-Never Land this time? Or, I hear they have some lovely rooms at the Back of the North Wind. All you need is a good imagination, Ivy dear," Frannie said.

They'd picked up their belongings and set off. "You can choose to live in a tree house, if you want to, like the Swiss Family Robinson. You are the only one who can decide."

"But will Papa find me there?"

"One day he will," Frannie said.

Darkness had fallen on the wet city streets. Ivy had no idea where it was they were headed. But she was relieved at Frannie's decision to take shelter from the rain for a while, stopping in at the diner where Gloria had recently been hired.

They'd found her busily scraping plates, carrying dishes into the kitchen, and wiping down tables. Gloria had brought them a pair of heavy, white china cups and a pot of tea, which she topped up with hot water or another tea bag whenever she passed their booth.

Frannie had used the telephone at the diner to call anyone she could think of who might know of a room to rent, and Ivy, who was only ten at the time, had fallen asleep with her head on the table.

It was Johnny, Frannie's boss at the bakeshop, who'd given them Mrs. Bingley's number. He'd even come and picked them up at the diner in his car and delivered them and their bundles to the rooming house. They had already begun to call the place Shangri-La.

Ivy had never ridden in a car before. She wished it weren't nighttime; she so much wanted the people on the street to see her. Johnny had helped them haul their things to an upstairs room, and before he left he'd given Frannie a meat pie from his bakery for their supper.

"You see how kind people can be, Ivy." Frannie had sliced the pie into little slivers. It would last two or three days out on the window ledge where it was cool.

"That is how you must behave, my darling. There are angels all around us, even when you least expect them."

Ivy stepped onto the sidewalk out front of Mrs. Bingley's. She looked back just once, and saw Lady Natalie of Bing watching her from the window.

She couldn't help feeling a little sad at leaving this place. She and her mother had lived in one of Mrs. Bingley's rooms for almost two years. It was the longest they'd ever lived anywhere.

Growing Up Ivy

Squaring her shoulders as best she could, considering the suitcase, Ivy took the first brave footsteps toward her new adventure. She'd need every one of Frannie's angels now.

3

Gloria

Inside the diner, Ivy slid the envelope across the table. "Momma said you'd go with me to my grandmother's. Fifty-four Arthur Road, Larkin, Ontario. I hope it's not too far."

Gloria frowned, studying the address. "You ever met your grandmother?"

"I don't think so. Have you?"

"Not this one. I knew Frannie's own folks, Mr. and Mrs. Johns. They were real nice. They both died of the diphtheria, and so did Frannie's only brother, little George. She ever tell you that? Frannie and I were just about your age when it happened, and we were best friends. Their house was quarantined and everything."

Ivy had heard the story before, but Frannie didn't believe a person should dwell on the sad things in life, so it was rarely mentioned. The only reason Frannie had escaped the same fate as that of the rest of her family was that her parents had sent her to stay with Great Aunt Charlotte in Guelph until the danger had passed.

There was no family left by the time it was deemed safe enough for Frannie to return. Instead, she remained in Guelph, where Aunt Charlotte's home became hers and where she finished her schooling. She was seventeen when she came back into Gloria's life again.

Before she died, Aunt Charlotte arranged for Frannie to be employed by Mrs. Hubert Hinkman, an old friend of hers back in Toronto. It wasn't long before Frannie had her own little flat and a few pieces of furniture. Shortly afterwards, she met and married Alva Chalmers, the man who would be Ivy's father.

Gloria held the envelope up to the light at the window. "I don't suppose your grandmother knows that you're coming," she said.

"I think she's going to be surprised," Ivy said. "Mostly everyone likes surprises, don't they? And the letter will explain everything to her. Do you know how far it is to Larkin?"

Gloria pocketed the letter and edged her slim body out of the booth. "Far enough that I can't take you today, Ivy. In fact, you're going to have to wait till my day off. Which isn't until Sunday."

Today was only Thursday.

"That's all right," Ivy said. "If I can just stay with you, I promise to be no trouble."

"Have you had anything to eat this morning?" Gloria swiped a damp cloth over the table.

Ivy told her about the doughnuts and the reason that she'd eaten both of them before going to bed.

After she'd spoken to someone in the kitchen, Gloria brought Ivy two plates of food. On one were two pieces of unbuttered toast. Ivy stared at the other, which held a greyish egg in a puddle of water.

"That's poached," Gloria said.

A dollop of ruby red jelly in a little paper cup came with the toast. "This is almost too beautiful to eat," Ivy said.

"Just spread it on the toast." Gloria reached into the booth behind her and, with a quick glance toward the kitchen again, produced a similar paper cup of orange marmalade. Frannie was right; Gloria Klein was an angel.

When the diner started to fill up with customers at lunchtime, Gloria took Ivy's coat and suitcase and set them behind the counter. "Shouldn't you be in school, Ivy? If you could go for the afternoon, I'd be finished here by the time you get out, and I'd take you back to my place."

"I'd just as soon not go to school, if you don't mind," Ivy said. "When I get to my grandmother's, I'll have to go to a different school anyway."

"Well, it's like this, Ivy." Gloria lowered her voice. "I can't have you taking up the seat of a paying customer. Not while we're busy."

Ivy had the feeling that the faceless person in the kitchen had something to do with this. But she couldn't bear to think that Gloria might get in trouble for her being there.

"I'll just go across the street and sit in the park," she said. "I went to that park once with Momma when I was little, and we had a lovely time."

She and Frannie had sat on the grass that day and pretended to have a fairy picnic, gathering leaves and acorns to use as tiny dishes.

The park seemed different now, with many of the benches occupied by jobless men playing checkers or stretched out sleeping with newspapers covering their faces. Ivy had forgotten how little grass there actually was, how few places for Frannie's fairies to hide.

She had to search for a vacant bench, one with

the least amount of pigeon droppings. For the rest of the afternoon, afraid of losing her bench if she left it, she watched the frantic scurrying of the squirrels, and imagined meeting her grandmother for the first time.

On the way home to Gloria's they stopped to buy a few groceries. While Gloria was making her careful selection, Ivy swirled about in the sawdust at the back of the store.

"Twelve cents a pound," the butcher said, when Gloria asked the price of round steak.

Ivy saw her finger the coins in her change purse. "We'll just take one of those sausages, please," said Gloria.

Ivy loved the pungent smell of ripe fruit in the store, and as a special treat, Gloria bought one beautiful, brown pear. When they arrived at the flat she cut it in half, then divided each half into eight slender sections. The pear was crisp and sweeter than anything Ivy could have imagined, sweeter even than the oranges that had come in their food hamper last Christmas. Frannie had called them "ambrosia."

The air in Gloria's flat was stale and smelled of cigarettes, although she'd told Ivy that the smoker, the former boyfriend, Eugene, was gone from her life.

"And good riddance to bad rubbish, is how I feel about that," Gloria said. She yanked some laundry off a line that was strung across the living room.

"Open the window if it bothers you. But sometimes the stink from the tannery comes way up here, and that's much worse."

Concerned that Ivy would be bored while she was at work for the next two days, Gloria found a pencil and some paper for her, suggesting that she might like to draw. Ivy thought she could find a much better use for the paper.

The next morning she picked up the pencil and began to write something that had been taking shape in her head ever since her mother left. She titled it *The Story of Ivy and Frances*. She would give it to Frannie when she came back from New York, and could already picture her delight at reading it.

Once Ivy started writing, the words tumbled easily onto the page. Except for getting up to wash the sink full of dirty dishes and to make herself a sugar sandwich, she worked on the story all day.

She was surprised when she finally looked up at the clock on top of the icebox to see that it was almost time for Gloria to come home. Ivy gathered her papers and was tucking them away when she heard Gloria's key turn in the lock.

Gloria collapsed into the nearest chair and kicked off her shoes. "Oh, my golly, am I bushed. What a day!"

She looked around with obvious pleasure at the tidy apartment. "I see you've been keeping yourself busy," she said. "I've never seen this place look so good. I just might have to keep you, Ivy Chalmers."

"I spent most of the time writing," Ivy said. "Once I got started, I couldn't stop. What do you suppose a person has to do if they want to be a writer, Gloria?"

Gloria covered a yawn. "I'm not sure, Ivy. Maybe it's like a lot of other things, and you have to just keep practising."

"That's what I'm going to do, then," Ivy said. "Every chance I get."

Gloria heated a can of soup on the hot plate for their supper, and they shared a currant bun, left over from the diner, for dessert.

Watching Gloria dunk her half of the bun into her tea to soften it, Ivy thought about what Gloria had said about keeping her. She considered asking if she could stay. If it weren't for the fact that her father would never find her here, she thought she could be happy living with Gloria Klein.

After Gloria left for work on Saturday, Ivy watched as the scene below the apartment window came to life — dozens of children playing noisy games of tag or kick the can up and down the street, adults sitting on the front steps of the rooming houses and shouting across to each other.

It was a familiar scene, but not one that Ivy had ever been a part of. Instead, encouraged by her mother, she had learned that she could be happy within the confines of a dreary room by escaping into her imagination. She turned from the window and picked up her story again.

When Sunday came, Gloria and Ivy boarded the streetcar, riding it to the end of the line. From there, they set out on foot to walk the rest of the way to meet Ivy's unsuspecting grandmother.

4

The Road to Larkin

Leaving behind the last of the small shops and houses that straggled to the outskirts of Toronto, the two travellers followed the highway out into the countryside.

They walked all morning, taking turns carrying the suitcase. Gloria had fashioned a strap and a handle for it from an old belt that had once belonged to Eugene.

By noon they were travelling between fields and farms where cattle grazed and curious horses came to watch. Until now, Ivy's encounters with animals had been limited to the delivery horses in the city and those she saw in the Agricultural Building at the Canadian National Exhibition. She'd quickly discovered that it was worth attending school on the last day each year, just to get the free pass to Children's Day at the Ex.

They stopped for a rest early in the afternoon, in the shade of a row of large trees that fronted the lush green of a golf course. Ivy flopped down and pulled off her shoes and socks, rubbing her bare feet over the cool grass and flexing her toes.

"I hate to ask you again, Gloria," she said, "but how much farther do you think it is?"

"The longest stretch is behind us now," Gloria promised. She tucked her cotton dress under her and sat down beside the girl.

The plaque on one of the stone pillars at the entrance to the golf course read SHADY DELL GOLF & COUNTRY CLUB. A group of men moved slowly across the clipped grass in the distance.

On the other side of the road, a teenaged boy wearing overalls and a cloth cap was walking back and forth in the wide ditch, his head lowered as if he was looking for something. Every once in a while he'd bend down and pick up some object.

When he reached the end of the ditch and came up on the same level as the road, Ivy saw that he carried a wire basket half filled with little white balls. The boy turned and retraced his steps, head down, combing the long grass with his eyes.

Ivy watched with great interest. Who was this boy? And where would he go when his basket was full and it was time to go home? Maybe he lived in Larkin, since they weren't too far from there now. He might even know her grandmother.

Gloria had gotten to her feet and was brushing off the back of her dress. "Best be on our way again, Ivy," she said. She poked at something with the toe of her shoe, and a golf ball popped up out of a depression.

"Here's another one," she called, and gave the ball a kick with the side of her foot, in the boy's direction.

The boy looked up to see it bouncing across the road toward him. With one sweep of his hand he captured it and dropped it into the basket.

Gloria and Ivy walked past, and he took off his cap a moment, revealing a thick mop of reddish-blond hair. "Thanks, Miss," he said, with a nod to Gloria. The skin on his bare shoulders was pink and peeling from the sun, his long arms covered in freckles.

Ivy was hoping that Gloria might ask him what he did with the balls he collected. Did someone pay him a penny or two for each one, the way the junk-man back home did for rags and bottles? But just then a red truck came rattling up behind them, diverting their attention.

Because it was Sunday, few vehicles had passed them thus far. The pair stepped to the side to let the truck, and the clouds of dust it was kicking up, go by.

To their surprise, the vehicle stopped and waited for them to catch up.

"Where you two ladies headed?" a friendly voice called out.

The driver was a man whose round, ruddy face peered out the window from under the brim of a straw hat. A dark-haired woman scowled at them from the passenger side of the seat.

Gloria set the suitcase down and stepped up to the truck's window. She showed the man the envelope she carried with Maud Chalmers's address on it. "We're going to Larkin," she said.

"Town's just down the road a piece," the man said. "Not too far now."

"I'm delivering Ivy here to her grandmother." Gloria put an arm around the girl's shoulders. "We've already spent most of the day walking. And then I have to turn around and get myself back to the city again."

"We're going right close to the street you're looking for. The missus and I are dropping in on a sick cousin of hers. If you two don't mind riding on the back, I can leave you off at the nearest corner. Get you there quicker 'n Shank's pony."

While he was talking, a dog that had been lying on the seat managed to shove his shaggy head out the window. The man pushed him away good-naturedly.

"Come on, Ivy," Gloria said, and, calling out her thanks, she steered Ivy around behind.

The back of the truck was open, with wooden side rails and a low floor. Gloria hoisted the suitcase onboard, and they hiked themselves up to sit on opposite sides so they could hang onto the rails.

"All aboard," Gloria said, with a wink.

"Momma would call this the most wonderful luck," Ivy said.

The dog was keeping an eye on them through the back window now, its red tongue lolling out. Ivy had no doubt that he was wishing he could trade places with them. Who wouldn't prefer to ride on the back?

She watched the boy back at the golf course fade into the distance.

5

Meeting Maud Chalmers

Ten minutes after picking up Ivy and Gloria outside the Shady Dell Golf Course, the red truck rolled to a stop at a street corner in the next village.

The driver came around to help them climb down from the back. "This is Larkin," he said. "This here crossroad is McCane. You'll find Arthur Road is one block over, before you get to the tracks." And to Gloria he said, "If you're right here in a couple of hours, Miss, you can ride back to the city with us."

"I'll be here," Gloria promised. She took hold of the strap on the suitcase again.

They found Number 54, halfway down Arthur Road, behind a picket fence. It was a two-storey house, grey and narrow, looking pinched between its neighbours. There were four slim windows in the front — two above a porch roof and two on either side of a green door.

Ivy immediately noticed the white lace curtains. She was used to window blinds in their rented rooms — vicious blinds that would snap back up out of reach or come off their rollers altogether when she tried to adjust them.

After knocking at the front door and receiving no answer, Gloria led the way along an alley no wider than a wheelbarrow that ran between the houses. The property at the back was only as wide as the house itself, but more than twice as deep.

Except for a shed in one corner, the yard was given over almost entirely to a vegetable garden. Someone had recently been planting in it, marking the rows with lengths of string attached to pieces of broken stick.

"Let me try, Gloria," Ivy said, when no one answered Gloria's knock. But though she rapped on the wooden door till it rattled in its frame and her knuckles were sore, she had no better luck.

They returned to the front porch and sat on the steps to wait, neither of them bold enough to occupy the single rocking chair that faced the street.

Gloria kept checking her watch, and Ivy knew she was afraid of missing her ride. She wished she could think of a way to keep her there. Maybe her grandmother would insist on putting on a big meal to celebrate Ivy's arrival and then, because it would be late, she'd invite Gloria to spend the night.

"I'm awfully hungry," Ivy said. She wrapped her skirt around her knees and imagined that big meal. Gloria had brought two currant buns for the journey, but Ivy had eaten hers the first time they'd stopped to rest.

"I expect you've been hungry before, Ivy," Gloria snapped, and after a moment, "Golly, I'm sorry. I didn't mean to bite your head off. I just don't know what to do, now that your grandmother isn't home. I can't just leave you here. What if she's gone out of town?" She opened her purse. "Here, you can have my bun."

"Oh, no, I couldn't," Ivy said. "I'm sure Grandmother will feed us. You haven't had a thing to eat yourself."

"Take it, Ivy." Gloria pressed it into her hands. "I'll be back home in no time and can eat all I want."

Following the direction Gloria's gaze had taken, Ivy saw someone coming along the broken sidewalk toward them — a tall woman with a long face and an angular figure, wearing a belted black dress. A small black hat sat on a head of greying hair.

Ivy wasn't sure about the Queen of Siam, but she knew instinctively that this was her grandmother, Maud Chalmers, dressed in her Sunday best. She tucked the bun into her pocket. She and Gloria got to their feet as the woman opened the gate.

"What's this now?" The woman pointed an accusing finger at the battered suitcase sitting on her front porch.

"Those are all my worldly possessions," Ivy said.

"And just *who* are *you*?"

"I'm Ivy Rose Chalmers, Ma'am. Your grand-daughter. I've come to stay for a while."

"Are you really?" Slowly the woman turned her glare on Gloria. "And who might this be?"

Gloria stuck out a confident hand. "My name's Gloria Klein. I'm an old friend of Ivy's mother, Frannie."

"Frances," Ivy said.

"Something happen to Frannie?" The tone of voice was sharp.

"No, Ma'am." Ivy spoke up quickly. "My mother's an actress now, you know, and she's gone to New York City to become a star. Gloria has a letter for you from her."

Maud Chalmers looked her visitors up and down for a long moment before sliding a finger under the flap of the envelope Gloria had handed her. She took out the letter, and as she read it, her frown deepened.

"Well, you might as well come in," she said, refolding the letter. "I don't intend to stand out here in this heat any longer than I have to."

In the small entranceway, Maud removed her hat, re-sticking it with its long pin and hanging it on a coat rack at the foot of the stairs. The newcomers stood by and waited. Ivy breathed in the scent of furniture polish, the fragrance of freshly ironed sheets.

Without another word, the woman strode down the hall to the kitchen at the back of the house. Ivy heard her running water into a kettle, heard it scrape on the stovetop as she set it to boil. By the time she returned to usher her visitors into the living room, she was shoving her arms into an apron that covered her dress from neck to hem.

"Sit there," Maud said, indicating a wooden settee. She took a chair on the opposite side of a low table.

"You do realize, don't you," she said, addressing Gloria, "that I have never before laid eyes on this girl? For all I know, she could be some street urchin, looking for free room and board."

Ivy sucked in a horrified breath and Gloria shrugged. "I guess you will have to trust me that she is not," she said.

"And you, Miss, are a complete stranger to me. Why should I trust you?"

"Because Gloria Klein is my mother's oldest and dearest friend," Ivy said. "Besides that, she is a perfect angel."

Clamping her hands over the arms of her chair, Maud failed to hide a bitter smile. "Well, the girl *sounds* exactly like her mother, anyway," she said.

After that, there seemed to be no further doubt about Ivy's parentage in Maud Chalmers's mind.

Because Gloria had to hurry now if she wanted to catch her ride home to Toronto, there was little time for conversation. Ivy choked down the cup of strong tea that was served in the kitchen, without sugar or ceremony.

Walking back with Gloria to the intersection, Ivy seized hold of her hand, swinging it playfully, but not wanting ever to let it go.

"Everything will be fine, Ivy," Gloria said. "I'm sure your mother would never have planned for you to live with someone who wasn't a good person." In her heart, Ivy knew this was true.

"But, Gloria, do you think my grandmother will turn out to have a good imagination?" she asked.

"What does it matter, Ivy?" Gloria said. "You have enough imagination for both of you. And after a while, you and your grandmother will learn to love each other. You'll see. Why, by the next time I come to see you …"

"Then you will come, Gloria? Please? Don't leave me here too long by myself."

"Of course, I'll come," Gloria said. "Just let anyone try to stop me."

In spite of Ivy's fervent wish that the man had forgotten his promise, the red truck appeared right on time. The dog was sitting upright in the middle of the seat, like the third member of the family. The missus scowled at the road ahead.

Ivy felt the prick of tears as she let go of Gloria's hand and watched her hop up onto the back.

The driver waved an arm out the window, and the truck pulled back onto the road. "Nice to meetcha, kid," he called.

Gloria was sitting on the back, one arm through the side rail, her bare, freckled legs swinging.

Ivy cupped her hands to her mouth. "Gloria!" she shouted. "Don't forget that I'm here!"

Ivy didn't know whether or not her mother's friend heard her, but the jaunty little salute Gloria sent gave her the courage to turn around and head back to whatever awaited her at the house on Arthur Road.

6

Camelot

Maud Chalmers was sitting on her porch in the rocking chair when Ivy turned the corner onto Arthur Road again. She could feel the woman's piercing gaze all the way down the sidewalk to the house. Never had her feet and legs moved so awkwardly, nor her arms seemed so skinny and long; it was as if they dangled below her knees.

"Well, this is a nice kettle of fish, isn't it?" Her grandmother confronted her before she'd reached the front steps. "Your mother's gone and left you."

"I knew she was going," Ivy said. "And she'll be back, like always. Usually, I just wait for her at home, but this time she wanted me to come here."

"And have you any idea just how long this wait will be?"

Ivy shrugged. "She didn't tell me. As long as it takes to become a star, I guess."

Perhaps to keep from saying anything she might later regret, Maud picked up the letter that had been lying in her lap and read it again. The rhythm of the rocking increased.

Lowering herself to sit on the top step, Ivy stared out at the street and the railroad track that ran along beside it. There were no houses on the other side of Arthur Road, only an untidy barricade of trees and bushes that failed to hide the assortment of garbage trapped underneath.

Eventually, the creaking of the rocking chair stopped and Ivy's grandmother got to her feet. "Well, I expect you're hungry," she said. There hadn't been so much as a crust of bread offered with the cup of tea that she had provided before Gloria left.

Following her grandmother down the hall to the kitchen, Ivy remembered the little waxed paper package in her pocket. She took it out and opened it. "Gloria gave me a bun," she said. "Why don't I just eat it, for now? Save you any trouble."

To Ivy's surprise, the woman snatched the bun from her and began to examine it, picking at one of the currants. Then, without another word, she tossed it into a pail that sat next to the sink.

Ivy blinked. "I could have eaten that."

"Three days old, at least," Maud said, and she set about to prepare a supper of sardines on toast, instead.

Ivy had always had to eat sardines with her eyes closed. She kept her head down, hoping that her grandmother wouldn't notice.

They ate in silence. Ivy felt as though her grand-mother had insulted her personally by rejecting Gloria's currant bun. When the meal was over, she carried her plate to the sink.

"My mother and I never waste food," she said. "She used to work in a bakeshop, and we always had three-day-old bread. It was still good, even if it was a little dry."

"You won't find me wasting food either, young lady. In fact, you may come with me in a minute and feed the contents of that pail to the chickens."

"You have chickens?" Immediately, Ivy felt her spirits lift. "Oh, may I see them?"

"Bring the pail along, then."

At the bottom of the garden, Ivy discovered ten brown hens pecking about in a pen attached to the side of the shed. They crowded around her legs as soon as she opened the wire gate, eager for the scraps she'd brought. Somehow it made her feel a little bet-ter to know there were other creatures living here with this formidable woman.

50

Ivy tore the currant bun into little pieces and scattered it for the hens. "While I'm here, can these chickens be my pets? I've never, ever had a pet before. They weren't allowed any place we lived, and besides, Momma had a hard enough time just keeping the two of us fed. And would it be all right if I gave the chickens names?"

Her grandmother looked on from outside the pen. "I can't say as I ever felt the need to name them," she said. "They're all exactly the same to me."

"Oh, I'm sure they're not. Look at how this one walks with a little limp. I think I'll call him Tiny Tim."

"It's a hen, Ivy; that means it's a female." With an exasperated flap of her apron, Maud turned back to the house. "But you do whatever you like," she said, over her shoulder. "Just don't expect me to call them anything but Chook. And I don't want any blubbering when one of them finds its way into the stewpot."

"Don't you worry," Ivy whispered. She closed the catch on the wire gate behind her. "I would never let that happen to a pet of mine."

Maud was waiting for her in the kitchen. "Bring that suitcase and come with me. We'd best decide where you're going to sleep."

"I can sleep anywhere at all," Ivy said. "I'm really no trouble, Momma says."

"Does she, indeed. Come along upstairs and we'll see about that."

There were two bedrooms on the second floor of the house, one behind the other, tucked under the slope of the eaves. Both were furnished with steel bedsteads that were covered by patchwork quilts, flattened and faded from years of washing.

Ivy crossed the gleaming linoleum at the top of the stairs to the room at the front. Besides the bed, there was a chest of drawers set between the two front windows. She lifted aside a flowered curtain in the corner of the room and found a small clothes closet, empty except for a few wire coat hangers.

The back room, with its single window, was just as plain as the one at the front. Ivy hesitated in the doorway between the two. "Which one is my father's room?" she asked.

"Good heavens, child! Is that what you were hoping? That he would be here? Your father hasn't lived in this house in years. There's no work in this town to keep him, or anyone else for that matter.

"And if you're worried about where I sleep," Maud said, "my bedroom is downstairs, to the left of the front door. You may choose whichever room you like up here."

"Really? I've never had a room all of my own." Ivy

looked into the woman's unsmiling face. "Just until my mother gets here, of course."

She went into the back bedroom again, unable to decide. If she slept in here, she could look down on her chickens and over into the backyards of the houses on the next street. She liked to watch people going about their lives. From this window, too, she could see all the way back to the road that would one day take her home to Toronto.

Ivy returned to the front bedroom. "But if I choose this one, I can watch the trains go by."

Before the girl could change her mind, Maud opened up the top drawers of the dresser, removed a few items and tucked them into the lower drawers. "I'm sure you can unpack your things yourself," she said. "I have something to tend to downstairs."

"Of course, Grandmother." Ivy lifted the suitcase onto the bed. Gloria had folded her blue coat and tucked it under the strap that held everything together. Thoughts of Gloria brought on a wave of homesickness.

Determinedly, Ivy gathered her nightgown, socks, and underwear and set them into the drawer. She would try to be brave, in order to face the new adventures ahead.

Hanging the coat and her other dress behind the

flowered curtain, she returned to the kitchen, where she found her grandmother greasing a cake tin.

"Looks like you're going to do some baking," Ivy said. "Is this a special occasion?"

"Possibly. But this is just a plain, rolled oat cake."

"Is it a special occasion because I'm here?" Ivy dared to ask.

"Well, I suppose it's not every day one has a grand-child come to stay," Maud said, but she didn't look up from the mixing bowl.

Ivy pulled a chair out and sat down to watch. "Momma thought we should pretend this town is Siam and that you are the dowager queen." She was feeling giddy with gratitude for the special cake, and there-fore, reckless.

"But I've decided that, since you live on a street named after King Arthur, I'm going to pretend this town is Camelot. Your house can be Arthur's castle. It sat on the peak of a hill, you know, overlooking a beautiful river."

Maud whacked the wooden spoon against the side of the bowl. "The only thing this house overlooks, Ivy Chalmers, is the railway tracks, and you'd best remem-ber to draw the curtains over your windows when you're undressing, else the engineers can look right in at you."

Ivy wanted to know everything there was to know about her father. What little bits of information she managed to extract from her grandmother were never enough to satisfy her. She was sure the reason Frannie had picked this place to send her, while she was making a name for herself in New York, was that it was the most likely place for Ivy's father to come looking for her.

A picture of mother and son, taken when the boy was about eight, hung in a shadowy corner of the dining room. It was the only picture Ivy had ever seen of Alva Chalmers, and in it he was even younger than she was now.

Studying its sepia tones, Ivy saw where her dark hair and eyes had come from. She'd also inherited his small, turned-up nose and short upper lip that didn't quite cover the front teeth.

The boy in the picture looked uncomfortable. He was wearing a sort of sailor suit and white stockings. He stood very straight beside his mother, neither one touching the other.

He had been Maud's only child. He'd gone to the school here in Larkin — the same school Ivy would attend if she stayed long enough (and Ivy was quite sure that she would not).

With the death of the boy's father, Maud's husband, it had been necessary for Alva to leave school and go to work in the woollen mill to help support the two of them. While he was still in his teens, the mill had closed, and Alva had moved to another factory job, this time in Toronto.

"I suppose Papa must come and visit you sometimes," Ivy said hopefully. Otherwise, how was he ever to know that she was there, waiting for him?

She was standing on a kitchen chair while Maud pinned up the hem of a dress one of the church ladies had given her for the girl. It was a horrible dress, in Ivy's opinion — purple, with little fuzzy knobs all over it. But since she did not intend to be here long enough for anyone to get to know her, she would grit her teeth and wear it.

"Your father is a busy man, Ivy," Maud said, taking a pin from between her lips. "He has no time to visit. He sends me what he can by money order every month, to help with the upkeep of this place."

"Then, couldn't you write and tell him about me? Tell him that I am here and dying to meet him?"

"Somehow, I hardly think you'll die from lack of seeing him. Your mother never made the least effort that I know of.

"There, that does it. Take the dress off, Ivy, and bring it back down to me."

"I can already tell it's going to be itchy," Ivy muttered, when she was halfway up the stairs.

While Ivy waited for Frannie's return, the lives of the two residents of 54 Arthur Road began to follow a predictable pattern. Every day, unless it rained, Ivy watered the rows of vegetables in the garden behind the house. She learned to prime the pump in the yard, pouring a little water into the top of it first, then working the handle up and down, up and down, till she felt it take hold, raising the water up from the depths. The watering can sat under the spout, ready for the first gush of water.

She'd been amazed to see how quickly the radishes, which Maud told her had been planted the day before she arrived, began to poke through the earth, and how the beans seemed to grow taller, almost overnight. Unfortunately, the weeds did the same, and there was always the endless job of hoeing.

First thing each morning, Ivy fed her chickens and collected the eggs from the henhouse, a sectioned-off area inside the shed. Having to shoo the chickens off their nests made her feel bad, and she always apologized for taking their warm eggs.

"Don't be silly," Maud said. "Times are hard. I've

got regular customers who pay me twelve cents a dozen for those fresh eggs."

Every day after breakfast, Maud hung her apron on the back of the kitchen door, clamped her hat on her head, and marched to the lower end of the street to attend mass at St. Basil's-on-the-Corner.

Feeling both guilty for not going with her grand-mother, and curious to see what the inside of the church might look like, Ivy accompanied her one morning, early in her stay.

To her surprise, in spite of its stained glass win-dows, the interior of the church was almost dark, lit only by the flickering orange light from rows of can-dles burning at the front. There were many strange smells, but the predominant one was of dampness — a sharp smell that bit the back of Ivy's throat. The still air was so chilly that Ivy didn't stop shivering until she was finally out in the June sunshine again.

"If you don't mind, Grandmother," she said. "I'd rather just stay home next time."

"Suit yourself," Maud said. It was such a quick response that Ivy decided her grandmother was afraid that continued exposure to the cold church would cause her to get sick. Her grandmother wouldn't want that on her conscience when her father finally found her.

7

The Family Record

Ivy was finding it harder and harder to keep the game of "let's pretend" going in her mind. Instead of living in Camelot, life with her grandmother had a way of jarring her back to reality. She missed her mother's nightly stories and longed for something to read.

The only book Ivy ever saw in Maud's house was a big old Bible that suddenly appeared one afternoon on the table in the kitchen. Her grandmother had gone up the street to deliver some eggs, so Ivy sat right down and opened the book.

She was both horrified and fascinated by the many scary illustrations scattered throughout the pages of the Bible — Abraham preparing to sacrifice his son, Isaac, on the altar of wood; Samson pulling down the house of the Philistines on top of all the people gathered there.

Her grandmother had left a pencil in the middle of the Bible, where there was a special section called "Family Record." Ivy read what had been entered there with great interest:

"This is the Family Record of Maudie Stricker."

How long ago had her grandmother started keeping the record? The handwriting of that first sentence looked as if it had been done by a child.

Under the heading "Births," a new notation had been pencilled in at the bottom. The record of family births began, "Maud Ilene Stricker, Feb. 5, 1872," in the childish hand.

Then, in ink, "Arnold Chalmers, Apr. 25, 1874," followed by "Alva Stricker Chalmers, May 1, 1896."

That would be Papa.

There was another page, headed "Marriages," and under it, "Maud Ilene Stricker & Arnold Chalmers, June 4, 1892" and "Alva Stricker Chalmers & Dottie (Dorthy?) Bailey, January, 1917."

Who was Dottie Bailey? And how could she possibly be married to Papa?

Then came, "Alva Stricker Chalmers & Frances Mary Johns, November, 1917."

These were Ivy's parents. But the previous entry

meant that Papa must have been married for a few months to someone else, before he married Frannie.

The next page, headed "Deaths," provided the explanation. There were two entries: "Arnold Chalmers, 1906" (Ivy's grandfather) and "Dottie Bailey, 1917."

So, Papa's first marriage had ended in Dottie's death. That was sad, certainly. But had it not happened, he would not have married Frannie, and Ivy would never have been born.

Ivy turned back to the "Births" section, smiling to herself at the latest entry in Maudie Stricker's family record: "Ivy Rose Chalmers, August 13, 1918."

At times, Ivy felt so insignificant that she suspected she might be invisible. But seeing her name on this page was acknowledgement of her existence.

This last notation must have been the reason for Maud's bringing the Bible to the kitchen table that afternoon. Ivy closed the book, thinking more than ever now that there were many things she didn't know about her Papa.

From the very beginning, Maud had made it plain that she considered cultivating one's imagination a waste of time. But when she discovered that Ivy could be kept content for hours on end writing stories, she made sure that the girl was never without a stub of a pencil and some paper.

Along with string, boxes, jars, and elastic bands, Maud Chalmers saved every scrap of blank paper she got her hands on, even opening out any envelopes that arrived in the mail, in order to use the clean surface on the inside. She willingly shared this supply of paper with Ivy.

One morning Maud returned from St. Basil's to find, as usual, Ivy bent over her writing on the top step of the front porch. She stopped at the foot of the steps and scowled. "Don't you ever go to school?"

Ivy could tell by the way her grandmother had come limping up the sidewalk that her bunions were bothering her. She wished she hadn't added to the woman's misery by telling her, before she left for mass, that something had chewed off a whole row of cucumber vines in the night. No wonder her grandmother was feeling cross.

"I've been to lots of different schools," Ivy replied. She studied the writer's callous she was developing on the middle finger of her right hand. "I know all about King John and the Magna Carta, and I already know my twelve times tables, by heart. Want to hear them?"

Maud ignored the question. "I think you should

take a walk over to the school after lunch," she said. "Just so's you'll know where it is, when the time comes."

"Seems sort of silly for me to start school now," Ivy said, trailing behind her grandmother, into the house. "Won't it soon be out for the summer?"

Slipping her arms into the wraparound apron in the kitchen, Maud's gaze fell upon the empty dish rack beside the sink. Ivy had dried the breakfast dishes that she'd left there and had put them all back into the cupboard.

"That's true enough, I suppose," the woman conceded. "Likely won't hurt you to miss the last day or two."

They did take a walk together one afternoon, when Maud's feet were less painful, in the direction of the stone school that sat at the end of the main street. Before they got there, however, Ivy discovered a library, halfway down the block.

"Why didn't you tell me there was a library in Larkin? Oh, Grandmother, this is one of my most favourite places in the whole world. Please, let's go in."

Maud had never been inside the building before but she agreed to accompany her. She even took a nickel out of her purse and bought the girl a library card. Then she went out and stood on the steps while Ivy chose her books.

"You might have left some for the other children, Ivy," Maud grumbled, eyeing the load her granddaughter was carrying.

"They only let me take five this time," Ivy said, "because I'm just new."

"Five? How are you going to read all those and do your chores, too?" There was no point in continuing their walk now. Burdened as Ivy was, they might as well just go home.

"If you were to go to school, Ivy," Maud said, when they turned in again at their own gate, "you might meet some children your own age."

A train was chuffing slowly down the track toward them, shaking the ground under their feet. Ivy hurried ahead to set her books on the porch steps and ran back to the fence to wait for it.

"Don't worry about me, Grandmother," she cried. "I've never needed other kids. I'm happy with you and the chickens. And now that I've joined the library, I'll never be lonely."

Maud opened the front door and disappeared inside.

The trains that used the single track on Arthur Road ran to a switch farther along the rails, where the rear cars were shunted onto a short line to the canning factory. They would be slowing down by the time they reached Maud's house, and Ivy liked to catch the eye of the engineer as he passed.

This time, both the engineer and the man hanging onto the last car, ready to unhook it, saw her and waved. Ivy turned with a satisfied smile to find Maud staring at her from the other side of the screen door.

"Stop wasting everybody's time, Ivy," she said. "I want you to get the basket and pick some lettuce for supper."

"Wouldn't you love to be going with them, Grandmother?" Ivy mounted the steps. "We could make believe they're headed for Samarkand and loaded with treasures from the Orient."

Maud held the screen door open for her. "I have no time for daydreaming. That train's just going to pick up a load of canned peas. You live in the real world, Ivy. The ones you and your mother created do not exist. And you both know it."

Ivy said nothing, but went to fetch the basket at the back door. Maud followed her, continuing her harangue.

"You might as well face facts, Ivy. You're almost thirteen, not a baby anymore. It's time to grow up. This is a harsh world you and I live in."

Ivy stepped back from the door so quickly that she trod on Maud's bunion. "Don't you think it was harsh for Momma and me, too? Every house we ever lived in was full of cockroaches. And sometimes we had to get into bed right after supper just to keep warm. We couldn't always afford to rent a room where the landlord would give us any heat. But nobody could stop us from pretending that things were better than they were."

Maud snorted. "The biggest fact you need to face up to is that your mother has deserted you."

Ivy dropped the basket and gaped at her grandmother for a full five seconds. How could anyone be so cruel? Let her pick her own lettuce! Ivy turned and fled upstairs to her room.

All the rest of the afternoon she waited there. She expected her grandmother to come up and apologize to her, imagined the sound of her footsteps on the stairs.

"Ivy, darling girl," she would say. "I'm so sorry. That was very unkind of me. Sometimes, the words just pop out of my mouth before my brain can stop them. Please forgive me."

But the voice in Ivy's head belonged to Frannie, not her grandmother. And her grandmother never came.

8
The Rescue

"There! I knew she would write!"

On the last day of June, after living at her grandmother's house for the best part of a month, a letter finally arrived for Ivy.

She picked at the glued flap on the envelope with anxious fingers, until Maud slapped a knife on the table in front of her. "Slit it open, Ivy. Don't destroy it."

Ivy withdrew a single, folded sheet of paper and let the envelope flutter to the table.

Dearest Ivy,

I miss you so much, darling girl. I hope you are having a fine time in Siam with your grandmother. Remember to treat her with respect. I know you will be kind to each other.

Did you find a school close by? A library, too, I hope, so that you can have lots of new adventures.

I am having the loveliest time here. You should see how many theatres there are. New York City is such an exciting place. I saw the Statue of Liberty and the Empire State Building, and even had a ride on the Staten Island Ferry.

The streets are crowded with people hurrying here and there. And all the tall buildings — they really do seem to scrape the sky. Not that I get much time to spend looking at the sights. One day you must come here, and we'll spend days and days just craning our necks.

The director has found a new play for me that will open later in the summer. I am to have the lead role, and judging by the crowds in this city who flock to the plays, I will soon be famous.

Stay healthy, my darling. Remember that with your imagination you can be wherever you want to be.

Your loving Momma,
Frances.
xxxxxxxxxxx

Ivy read the letter a second time, this time out loud.

"Momma sounds very happy, doesn't she? But she's forgotten to put her new address in the letter." Ivy picked up Frannie's envelope. "There's no address here either. How could she forget? I was supposed to write her back."

"Maybe your mother's not quite settled in one place yet," Maud said.

"That must be it." But it was hard to swallow her disappointment. Ivy had been composing letters to Frannie in her head ever since she arrived.

Ivy had been on her way out to fill the water trough for the hens when the mail arrived, so now, with her letter in her pocket, she opened the back door to go finish the task. Out of the corner of her eye, she saw Maud drop Frannie's envelope into her basket of scrap paper.

❧

As Ivy was returning from the library a few days later, her bag of books knocking gently against her bare legs, she came upon a peculiar sight out front of her grand-mother's house.

It was a covered wagon, built like the ones she'd seen in books that told how the American pioneers had travelled west. Except that the material stretched over the ribs to form the roof of this wagon had been painted blue and green and was daubed here and there with garish orange spots.

To Ivy's mind, it looked like something that might belong to a travelling magician. She hung her book bag on the picket fence and ventured over for a closer look.

A large grey horse stood harnessed to the front of the wagon, and the animal was nibbling on the grass that grew between the road and the tracks. Keeping a safe distance, Ivy circled the strange contraption.

There was a window in the back of the wagon and a stovepipe that stuck up through the roof. A two-wheeled cart was attached behind, its contents hidden beneath a canvas sheet.

At the front of the wagon, above the horse, there was a wide seat for the driver. Two wooden doors were hooked open behind it. Ivy craned to see inside, but from street level it was impossible.

Who did all this belong to? Since it had stopped out front of Number 54 Arthur Road, could the owner of the mysterious wagon be inside?

Entering the front door of her grandmother's house, Ivy saw someone sitting in the kitchen at the end of the hall. Because of the bright sunlight coming through the window behind him, she saw him only in silhouette.

Maud was standing at the sink, scraping carrots. Her back was to the visitor, a clear indication to Ivy that the man drinking tea at the table was no stranger. She set the book bag down with a clunk, and Maud fixed her with her usual glare. The man studied Ivy with a careful smile.

"Well, this here's the girl, Alva," Maud said, and wiped her hands on her apron.

"So it is." The man rose halfway to his feet and then sat down again, as if his legs had suddenly given out on him.

"This here's your father." Ivy's grandmother was addressing her.

Her father?

Ivy froze. This slight, rumpled man with the dark hair that began well back of his forehead, whose calloused hands gripped the table in front of him, was her father? This wasn't the way it was supposed to happen. Where was the white charger?

"Papa?"

Could it be?

71

The man nodded and cleared his throat nervously. "I don't know about the Papa part," he said. "But I'm your dad, all right."

Ivy's mouth fell open. She sank down onto the chair beside his and stared at him, noticing the narrow, rounded shoulders, the off-white shirt buttoned around a thin neck where a few untrimmed whiskers grew.

"You'll be catching flies like that, Ivy," Maud said.

A smile began to creep across Ivy's face. "I *told* Grandmother that one day you'd come and find me."

"Well, it's more an accident than anything," the man said. His speech was gentle and unhurried. "I just dropped in because I was coming this way and ..." He hesitated, then shook his head, as if he realized that he was about to spoil the girl's pleasure at their meeting. "And here you are!"

For a long moment they both sat there, taking each other in. It was as if they were the only ones in the room.

"So." Alva Chalmers was the first to speak. "Mother tells me Frannie's gone off on her own."

"That's just till she gets to be a star," Ivy said. "She's an actress, you know. One day she's going to be famous. Then she'll come home and be able to get all the parts she wants."

The man who was her father didn't argue the point the way her grandmother might have, and Ivy felt grateful to him for that.

"Is that your wagon out there?" she asked.

"Well, the owner called it a caravan. I've rented it for the summer. The big wagon's all fitted out inside, so a body can live in it while he travels around the country."

"It's very colourful," Ivy said. "It made me think it might be a magician's wagon."

"No, it's only a traveller's wagon."

"And that's your horse?"

"She's mine now. Her name's Dora. Would you like to meet her? I'm sure she'd be very happy if you were to take her one of Mother's carrots."

Still chewing on long strands of grass, Dora swung her head to watch the girl approach. She seemed to sense that Ivy had something for her, and she tried to get close enough to take it.

The horse made hollow, snuffling noises, her lips peeled back from big, yellow teeth. Afraid that Dora might take her fingers along with the carrot, Ivy tossed it onto the ground in front of the horse's hairy front hooves and stepped away.

Back in the kitchen, her father was just getting up from the table. "Did Dora say thank you?"

"Oh, I didn't know she was a talking horse," Ivy said. Could she have found in this man a kindred spirit? "We could pretend that she is."

"Don't encourage the child, Alva," Maud said.

"Well, now." Ivy's father pushed his chair back into the table. "I'd best be off, Mother. Dora and I have to put in a few miles before my first call. Thanks kindly for the tea."

"You're leaving?" Ivy was bewildered. "Then you didn't come here to get me? To take me with you?"

Her father frowned. "I didn't even know you were here, child."

"But I *could* go with you, couldn't I?"

When neither adult spoke, Ivy plunged on. "I had a letter from my mother the other day, and she's going to be busy all summer long in New York with her new play. There's really nothing keeping me here. Nothing at all."

Her father looked helplessly from Ivy to his mother and back again.

"Your father's a peddler, Ivy. Hardly the life for a young girl."

"I'm used to a hard life. Can't I go with you? Please, Papa. I'm no trouble at all. I love to read and write stories. You'd hardly know I was there."

Maud was suddenly struck with a fit of coughing.

74

"Really, Papa. I'm very quiet, and I know I could learn to love Dora. Even if she's not the fine white charger I imagined you'd be riding when you came to rescue me."

"Rescue you!" Maud had recovered. "There's no end to this child's imagination, Alva."

Ivy's father removed a wrinkled suit jacket from the back of the chair and picked up the hat that lay on the table. "She sounds for all the world like her mother," he said. But he said it kindly.

"I'll be away all summer, Ivy. A long ways from here. There's no conveniences in the caravan. And you might want the company of another female from time to time. Someone to talk about, well, womanly things."

He was turning the hat around in his hands, and Ivy saw his face redden. "It'll just be me and the horse till we get to the travellers' meeting in August. There'll be kids there, I guess."

"I don't need kids, Papa. And as for female company, I already know all about the womanly things you're talking about. Momma explained all about it, before I even started getting the monthlies. I can look after myself; you can be sure of that."

"Ivy! Mind your tongue!" Maud looked horrified.

"But he's my father. He knows about such things."

"Of course, Ivy," Alva said. He chewed at his lip while he considered her proposal. "There's room enough in the caravan, I guess. It might be kind of nice to have some company. But you'll find I'm not much of a talker."

"That's all right, Papa," Ivy said.

"She does the talking, most of the time," Maud said.

"Well, Mother? What do you think? You're probably ready for a rest now anyway."

"Oh, she is," Ivy said. "She'll be happy not to have to listen to all my idle chatter. Won't you, Grandmother?"

"I was counting on some help with the preserving," Maud said. "But I've never had any before, so why should this summer be any different?"

That appeared to settle it. But when Ivy ran upstairs to gather her clothes for the journey, Maud was right behind her.

"There are some things we do not mention in mixed company, Ivy." She opened the drawers of the dresser while Ivy pulled her old cardboard suitcase out of the chimney corner and flopped it onto the bed.

"I know you can look after yourself. But stop and think before you speak. Your father is a man. A good man, to be sure, but still a man."

Ivy transferred the contents of the dresser to the bed, and together they sorted and folded the clothing into the suitcase. Maud shook her head over all the mends in the girl's supply of underwear.

"There's another pair of bloomers downstairs, wanting some elastic. If your father can wait five minutes, I'll thread it through. But you'd best take lots of safety pins with you."

She lifted the curtain on the closet and removed the purple dress from its hanger.

"Not that dress, Grandmother," Ivy said. "I can't let Papa see me in that."

"Nonsense. Do you think for one minute that he cares what you look like? This dress is nice and cool, and you'll be able to rinse it out yourself. You'll be thanking me for it, one of these days, you mark my words."

There was no point in arguing; the hideous dress was already in the suitcase.

Before Ivy and her father could get away, Maud insisted on filling a basket for them with fresh vegetables from the garden — green beans, the last of the radishes, and some cucumbers.

"If I'd known you were coming, Alva," she said, pinching off some bright green lettuce, "I'd have had a chicken ready for you — though I'd likely have had a fight on my hands with the girl.

"Ivy, go back and see if there are any eggs. Might as well take whatever you can find."

"Don't worry, Mother," Alva was saying when Ivy returned with eight fresh eggs. "I've got enough food in the caravan for now. I hear tell that the customers will see that I don't starve. And they tell me the fishing's good along the way."

Alva received the eggs in his rough hands, and tucked them tenderly into the basket, down amongst the vegetables. "Off we go then, Ivy. Say goodbye to your grandmother."

He watched as Maud allowed Ivy to plant a kiss on her cheek. In return, his mother touched the girl's shoulder briefly. "I'll bring her back before the snow flies," he said.

"Absolutely not!" Maud had followed them out onto the front porch. "That girl's got to go to school in September."

Alva hesitated, rubbing a hand over his chin. "Can't really say where I'll be in September, Mother. We *could* be heading back this way."

"This is important, Alva. I didn't force her to go to school when she got here last month; she's a bright enough child. But she's got to start soon's you can bring her back. You mind now, Ivy. We don't want the truant officer coming around."

"Fine, fine," Alva said. "And if the sales are as good as I hope, Mother, there'll be some cash money to help you with your winter expenses. And Ivy's, too, of course. What I've left you today should get you a load of wood, at least."

"Oh, I won't be here in the winter," Ivy said. "My mother will be home long before that."

Dora watched as the three crossed the road in her direction, carrying Ivy's bags and the basket of provisions. The man tossed some bundles up onto the wagon and spoke in a low tone to the horse.

Ivy kept a close eye on Dora while her father hoisted her up to the seat. "She's not a wild animal, Ivy," Alva said. "She's a domestic creature, a horse as gentle as any you'll find."

"I know, Papa."

In her excitement at the prospect of spending the summer with her father, Ivy hadn't thought to ask what goods they'd be peddling around the countryside. When she scrambled over the seat and into the wagon, she discovered boxes and boxes of new shoes stacked on both sides of the caravan. And when she asked about it, her father told her that there were more bags of footwear in the two-wheeled cart they were pulling behind.

"Once we sell everything in the cart, we'll be leaving it off somewhere," Alva said. "We can travel faster that way, and we'll pick it up again on the way home."

He carried the old suitcase along the narrow aisle to the back of the caravan. "The bench under the window lifts up," he said. "There should be room for your things in there."

No sooner had they climbed back out and settled on the wagon seat, than Dora sensed that the time had come to be off. The man had only to pick up the reins, and the horse began to move forward.

Ivy waved at her grandmother, standing at the edge of the road. "Goodbye, Grandmother. We're off on a wonderful adventure."

"Oh, my goodness!" Maud suddenly flapped her hands. "Alva, wait just a minute!" And she went rushing back to the house.

"Whoa," the man spoke to the horse. "I guess we forgot something, Ivy. Whoa, Dora. 'Fraid I don't know how to back this thing up."

Ivy leaned around the edge of the caravan until she saw her grandmother trotting alongside, waving a brown paper bag.

"Ivy," she gasped. "I wanted you to have this. I bought it special, for your birthday. But seeing's how you won't be here, you should take it with you."

A birthday present. Ivy couldn't remember the last time anyone had given her a real present for her birthday, something that came from a store.

"You going to open it?" her father asked. But Ivy knew that he wanted to get going; she'd delayed him already by at least an hour.

"Oh, you can open it anytime," Maud said. "Get away with you now." She turned on her heel and strode back across the road.

Consumed with curiosity, Ivy unrolled the top of the brown paper bag and peered inside. To her amazement, what she lifted out was a thick writing tablet — hundreds of sheets of clean, lined paper — and a brand new pencil, its lead already sharpened. On the cover of the writing pad, Maud had printed IVY'S STORYS.

Opening the book's cover, she smoothed her hand over the first pristine page, smiling to herself and thinking of all the things she would write. But not yet — for now, she would hold the birthday present tight against her heart until they had left the town of Larkin far behind.

9

Revelations

"Don't forget to make a wish on the first star you see tonight, Papa," Ivy said, before climbing into the back of the wagon at dusk. "My wish has already come true."

How could she be any happier? Her father had found her at last; her mother — missing Ivy terribly — was following her dream in New York; and her grandmother, by giving Ivy a book in which to write her stories, had shown that she understood.

For the next two months the cozy caravan would be her home. Her bed was a hammock, slung along the aisle between the walls of shoes that gradually, over the summer, would shrink to nothing.

Alva had assured her that he'd be comfortable sleeping on the bench under the back window.

Ivy was lulled to sleep by the swaying of the hammock, the creak of the wagon, and the rhythmic clop, clop of Dora's hooves on the hard surface of the road.

Then, before she knew it, it was morning. Sometime during the night the caravan had stopped. Ivy swung down from the hammock and pushed open the doors behind the wagon seat.

Dora had been unhitched and was now tethered loosely to a tree, where she nibbled grass in the shade. Alva was crouched over an open fire. The aroma of frying eggs made Ivy's cheeks ache in anticipation.

"Good morning, Papa," she called. "I didn't hear you get up." She jumped down onto the dewy grass. "I started to make up a poem in my head last night. But now that I'm awake, it's gone."

Alva turned with a slow smile. "Well, I don't need to ask you if you slept good," he said. "Come and join me. There's a real nice stream just down the bank there. How do you like your eggs?"

"Any way but poached," Ivy said.

Maud would not have approved of the fact that she hadn't changed into her nightgown before climbing into bed last night. All it took this morning was a quick splash of cold water, and Ivy was ready to choose a brown egg for her breakfast and to start her first day on the road with her father.

"I'm so happy, Papa," she said. "I can't think of anything I'd rather do while I wait for Momma, than to spend the time with you. It's going to be a perfect summer. I can just feel it."

Although she knew by his own admission that Alva was not a great conversationalist, Ivy was curious to find out where he'd been all her life. It might take a while, but gradually the story would come out. She was sure of that. They had the whole summer to get to know each other.

When he told her that for the past two years he'd worked in a shoe factory, Ivy understood the stained and calloused hands.

She pictured him sitting astride a cobbler's bench, wearing a leather apron and skillfully wielding a small hammer, exactly like the illustration in the book of fairy tales.

This past spring, Alva had lost his job at the shoe factory. And then the peddling route had come available.

"That's the way it is with luck sometimes," Ivy said. "Have you noticed? All of a sudden, just when you need it, you'll have the most wonderful luck."

The man who'd had the route previously had grown tired of the life. Alva had bought Dora and rented the caravan from him, and the owner of the shoe factory had agreed to stock it, as he had in the past.

"But I paid for all the shoes that are in the small cart myself," Alva said. "So when I sell that lot, it's all money in my pocket."

"I can't imagine anyone growing tired of this life," Ivy said. "Can you?"

Already that morning they had stopped to let a large turtle dawdle across the road in front of them. A mile or two farther along, it was a spotted fawn and its mother, tiptoeing over the road to sample the grass on the other side. Ivy held her breath in delight. They watched the pair of deer until they slipped like shadows into the trees.

Alva smiled at Ivy. "I bet you could write a poem about that, now."

"Maybe you could, too, Papa. Do you like to write, like I do?"

A long silence. Then, "Well, it's like this, Ivy. I'm not very good at letters and such."

"Letters?" Ivy said. "Do you mean the alphabet?"

"I know my ABCs. Just not so many of the words they make when you string them together, like."

"You mean you can't write?" Ivy was wide-eyed.

"Nope. 'Fraid not. Not much of a reader, neither."

"Oh." Ivy looked at her father with sorrow. "I don't think I ever met anyone who couldn't read or write. Not a grownup, anyway."

"Well, now you've met one," he said.

"Oh, Papa, I'm sorry." She leaned forward so that she could look into his eyes. "I didn't mean to hurt your feelings. I'm sure you just never had the chance."

"True enough." Alva flapped the reins. "But learning came hard for me, the short time I did go to school."

"Papa, I have the best idea. I'm going to write you a story. I'll read it to you, and guess what, Papa? I will teach you to read it all by yourself. At first, I'll use only little words in the story. Like we had in our primer."

"Well now, Ivy. I don't know. It isn't easy to teach someone to read. 'Specially not someone as old as me. Nor as set in his ways."

"You're not set in your ways, Papa. You took on this peddling route, didn't you? That was a new adventure for you. I'd say it was very brave. And then you said your daughter, who you didn't even know, could come along with you. Anyone as brave and adventurous as you can learn to read."

"Well, now."

"Never mind," she said. "Just you wait and see!"

10
Life on the Road

"I think Dora remembers the regular stops along this route," Ivy said one day. "Don't you, Papa? From all the times she's travelled this way before."

Whenever the caravan approached a house or a farm gate beside the road, Dora's pace would slow, as if she were anticipating Alva's command.

"She is a very smart horse," Alva agreed. This mode of travel was a new experience for him, and he'd admitted to Ivy his relief at discovering a natural bond between himself and the animal.

At each stop they made, Ivy was expected to remain with Dora, while Alva went to knock on doors and talk to whomever answered. She got to know, just from the way he walked back to the wagon, whether or not he'd made a sale.

At times, her father's gait was slow, as if his feet were too heavy to lift. Without a word, he'd climb back up to the seat, give the reins a flick, look over at Ivy, and shake his head. Other times, Alva's stride was light and brisk, and he'd be wearing a smile as he made his way back to the wagon. He'd have with him a list of the shoe sizes the housewife had asked to be shown.

Reading numerals was not a problem for Alva Chalmers. He would simply match the ones on his list with those marked on the ends of the shoeboxes, and together he and Ivy would carry them up to the house.

Ivy kept her fingers crossed that every order would be a big one, so that her help would be required. This usually got her inside the door of the house, where she could catch a glimpse of the way the family lived.

Back in the city, she'd always welcomed an excuse to go walking at night with Frannie, looking in through lighted windows, imagining what secrets might lie in the rooms beyond their view.

Alva tried to keep the caravan on the small country roads where the cars were fewer, avoiding the highways wherever he could. Dora maintained a steady, unhurried pace, leading them onto the shoulder of the road if the drivers behind them started honking their horns.

The caravan drew curious stares everywhere they went, and if there were children around, they could be counted on to come running for a better look at the colourful contraption.

"What kind of a wagon is this, anyway?"

Ivy sat proudly erect on the seat. "It's a caravan."

"Are you folks gypsies, then?"

"I like to pretend that we are. But truly, we're just regular people."

"Can we look inside?"

It was evident from the awe in the voices that every child who took a peek inside Ivy's house-on-wheels wished they could trade places with her — *"Say, do you folks really live in here?"*

As she had predicted, Ivy grew to love the gentle Dora. It wasn't long before she was the one who led the horse to the place she would be hobbled for the night, after Alva had unhitched her from the wagon.

No longer did Ivy fear getting nipped when she stroked Dora's nose or fed her a handful of oats. "Hold your palm flat, Ivy," Alva had said. "So's your fingers don't get in the way of her teeth."

Ivy was sure that her father must be wondering what she was writing, all those endless hours spent beside him on the wagon seat — even though he seemed to show no interest in it whatsoever.

"Want to know the name of the story I'm working on this morning?" she asked.

"All right," came the indifferent reply.

"It's called 'The Story of Ivy and Frances.' I actually started it when I was at Gloria's, but I forgot those pages back at her place."

It was impossible to gauge her father's interest, because his expression didn't change. He kept his eyes fixed on the road ahead.

"It's about Momma and me and some of our adventures."

Still nothing from Alva.

Ivy had come to believe that her father was just too polite to question her about the last twelve years of her life. It seemed only natural that he'd be curious.

"Before Mrs. Bingley's, Momma and I moved quite a bit," Ivy continued. "One time, when the rent money was overdue, and the landlady was banging on the door of our room, the only way out was through the window. Would you like to hear what I wrote about that?"

Without waiting for an answer, Ivy began reading:

> *Someone was pounding on the door. Ivy and her mother, Frannie, knew it was Mrs. Potts. "Get your things together, Ivy," Frannie whispered. Frannie's real name was Frances.*

Frannie put everything into their suitcase and two of Mrs. Potts's pillowcases.

"I gave you fair warning, Mrs. Chalmers," said Mrs. Potts, who was still on the other side of the door. "I can rent this room to someone who can pay me on time."

"Someone who likes rats and roaches," said Frannie. She pushed the window up and set their things out onto the fire escape. "Come on, Ivy," she said.

Ivy watched her mother climb over the windowsill. Ivy was a little frightened because she was only six years old. But as long as Frannie was with her she knew everything would be all right. So Ivy climbed out the window too.

In a minute her mother was standing down on the ground with the suitcase. Ivy climbed slowly down the iron stairs. But when she got to the last one she saw that there was only a rope between the end of the fire escape and the ground.

"Toss me the bundles, Ivy," Frannie said, and Ivy did. "Now jump."

"It's too far," cried Ivy. "I'm scared."

"There's nothing to be scared of. I am right here to catch you."

Mrs. Potts had her head out the window upstairs and was shouting at them.

"Jump, Ivy," Frannie kept saying. "Close your eyes. Pretend that you are Tinker Bell and that you can fly. Come on now."

"I'm sending the bailiff after you!" Mrs. Potts yelled. "You can't get away without paying!"

Ivy closed her eyes and flew into her mother's arms, knocking her down when she landed. They both rolled over and over on the ground. No one was hurt, and soon they were both laughing. They picked up their bundles and walked away to find a new place to live.

Alva Chalmers was shaking his head as if he couldn't believe what he'd just heard, but he said not a word.

"Well, do you think it's a good story?"

"Is it the truth, or a made-up story?"

"Oh, no. It really happened. It's pretty funny, don't you think?"

"Funny? You said you were scared."

"Only at first. When it was all over we laughed and laughed. Momma found us another room, and one day we went back over to Mrs. Potts's with the money we owed her. And her two pillowcases."

Unexpectedly, Alva pulled back on the reins. "Whoa, Dora." The horse drew the caravan to the side of the road.

"We'll stop here and fill up the water jugs," Alva said. He climbed over the seat and into the caravan to collect the jugs.

"Frannie never *did* have much common sense," he said, before jumping to the ground.

Ivy passed the empty jugs down to her father and sank onto the seat again, the disappointment she felt at his reaction to her story mingled with confusion over his last remark.

It came as a cruel surprise to her that there were some stories she could not share with her father. The knowledge that she would have to be careful, to weigh what she told him, made her feel a little sad, as if she were cheating him out of part of her own story. Now she would tell him only what he wanted to hear.

It was a several minutes before Ivy could bring herself to join her father at the spring. She helped him carry the water back.

The July sun grew hotter and the roads more dusty. The ice in the caravan's icebox disappeared in no time, and they left a steady trickle of water on the dry road behind them.

Late each afternoon they would look for a place to stop for the night where they could take the washing-up bag and have a good soak in the cooling water of a lake or river.

Alva had learned from the previous owner of the caravan the location of the best streams to fish for brook trout that hid in the shadows of overhanging trees. Often, Ivy woke to find him cooking a sizzling pan of fish for their breakfast.

In the evening they stayed outside long after they had finished supper, letting the smoke from the fire keep the mosquitoes at bay. Only when the cool night air wrapped damp arms around their shoulders would they say goodnight to Dora, drop the bug netting over the doorway, and climb into their beds.

Ivy kept her mind busy day and night, thinking of the best way to help her father learn to read.

"You have to sound the word out, Papa," she said. "I know it's very confusing. The letter *C* has so many different sounds. In this word, *cat*, it has a hard sound, like *K*. Sometimes it depends what other letters are in the rest of the word. *CH* sounds different in *chicken* than it does in *character*. But don't worry; those aren't our words for today."

She worked at combining simple words into short sentences, and when her father had learned to recognize those words, they read the sentences together.

One night, near the end of July, she fell asleep to the satisfying sound of her Papa slowly reading the sentences that she had strung together that day to make a little story.

11
Anticipation

Ivy had been looking forward to the Travellers' Fair ever since her father first spoke of it. It was to be the climax of their summer adventure.

Every year, near the town of Birch Hills, on the first weekend in August, a large meeting of travelling salesmen would take place. From what Alva had been told, this gathering of peddlers, and however many family members they could muster, would camp together outside Birch Hills, setting out their wares so that everyone for miles around could come and search for a bargain.

"They tell me everyone has a grand time," Alva said. "The travellers sell to the public and trade amongst themselves, too. There'll be a real big party on the last night, to celebrate all the sales they've made over the weekend. Some folks bring musical instruments along. So, there'll be singing and dancing, too."

"A party, Papa? Does everyone get to go?"

"The whole camp, they tell me."

Even though she knew that when the fair was over Alva planned to head home again, Ivy began counting off the days. After the meagre sales of the last little while she was sure the event would help to buck up her father's flagging spirits. Sales on the road were not as good as Alva had expected.

"Seems like folks just aren't buying new shoes," he said to Ivy one day. "Everyone's just making do with what they have. Same as you and me, I guess."

"It's summertime, Papa." Ivy stretched her legs out and twiddled her bare toes. She hadn't worn shoes in days. "Wait till people start talking about the fall, or kids get ready to go to school again. It's sure to get better."

Sometimes Alva took pity on a family where one member really needed to have shoes to go looking for work, but had no money to pay for them. If their need was greater than his, he'd agree to barter, and he and Ivy would have fresh eggs for a while, or some crisp, red beets that tasted like the earth they came from.

"But tomorrow, it has to be a cash sale," Alva said one evening, as he peeled the skin off a boiled beet and plopped it onto Ivy's plate. She had to spear the slippery globe with her fork to keep it from sliding off onto the ground.

Brilliant red beets or a basket of warm biscuits, no matter how mouth-watering, would not make up for the pair of men's oxfords Alva would later have to pay for himself.

Each day now, as he walked back to the wagon after making a call, Alva's pace grew slower and slower. He'd climb back up to the seat as if that climb was the hardest thing in the world to do.

Ivy felt it was her job to administer cheering words. For weeks she tried to keep him optimistic that at the next farm, or on the next day, he would make a sale. "And just nine more days till the Travellers' Fair, Papa."

Before he and Ivy could settle into their beds each night, Alva insisted upon rearranging the boxes of shoes in the caravan. But no matter how they stacked them, the boxes still lined both sides of the wagon, and they had hardly made a dent in the load that was in the cart behind.

"It's bound to be better when we get to the fair next week," Ivy said. "I'm sure everyone will remember from other years that there will be a caravan filled with shoes for sale. Maybe they will even be waiting in line when we drive in."

They caught some little trout for supper one evening, at a stream that Alva had been on the lookout for. He cleaned the fish at the edge of the stream, burying the entrails before he and Ivy climbed back up to their campsite.

Almost tenderly, Alva laid the fish in a pan of flour, turning them once to coat their speckled sides. Watching the care he took in preparing their meal, Ivy felt a sudden rush of affection for him.

When Alva leaned over to set the fish in the frying pan that sputtered on the fire, Ivy put her head against his back.

"I love you, Papa," she murmured. She felt the muscles in his back tense.

"I'm not very good at all those love words," he said, and gave a small cough to cover his embarrassment.

"That's all right, Papa." She went and sat across from him on the round stones that circled the fire pit. Both father and daughter became intent on watching their supper cook. After a minute or two, Ivy ventured, "You loved my mother once, didn't you?"

"I did. Least, I thought I did."

"Then why, Papa? Why did you go away?"

"It wasn't like that, Ivy."

"Can you tell me about it, Papa?"

Alva flipped the fish in the pan, searing them on the other side. Ivy waited.

"I lost my first wife," he said slowly. "She came from a farm not too far from where I grew up." He sat down again on the stone.

"I never knew her then, though. Didn't meet her till she came to Toronto one time to visit a friend. Soon after, we got married — then she got real sick and she died."

He looked up at Ivy. "That's when I met your mother. She was so full of life, like a young kid. Frannie wanted to help me get over my grief. But after a while, I could see that I was just spoiling her happiness."

He took a deep breath. "It wasn't all bad. There was lots of work in those days, near the end of the war. I wasn't skilled at anything in particular, but I was never out of work, neither. Worked at a munitions factory for a while. Then we all heard talk that the best jobs to be had were in the mines up north. I had to go when I got the chance.

"Your mother had been working for a lady, and she didn't want to leave. Said a mining town was no place for a woman, and besides, she figured the nearest theatre would be hundreds of miles away. By then, Frannie was talking about being an actress. To tell the truth, Frannie and me had pretty much parted company by the time I left for the north. We had nothing in common anymore."

"Did you know about me, Papa?" Ivy hated to interrupt this unexpected flow of conversation, but had to know the answer all the same.

Alva's eyes were sad. "Believe me, child, I had no idea. Else I never would have gone.

"I did come back a couple of times, but Frannie was always too busy to see me. When I came back to Toronto for good, I tried looking for her. But like you said, she moved a lot.

"Then, purely by chance, about a year ago, I met her friend Gloria on a streetcar. She told me I had a half-grown daughter. I could hardly believe it."

"Did that make you happy?"

"You bet it did! I begged Gloria to tell me where you and your mother were living, but she'd promised Frannie she wouldn't. She did say that she would try to persuade Frannie to get in touch with me herself."

"And she never did?"

Alva shook his head. "I guess your mother wanted to keep you all to herself. Maybe she was punishing me. Maybe I deserved it."

He lifted the pan from the fire, balancing it on a stone. "Well, you can just imagine how surprised I was to get to Mother's last month and find you there."

"It was the best surprise ever," Ivy said. "For both of us."

When the fish were ready, Ivy passed Alva the tin plates. "I really think, Papa, that in her heart, Momma wanted us to meet."

Alva slid one of the fish onto Ivy's plate. "I don't know, Ivy. You can think that if it makes you feel better. It was always hard for me to figure out what was going on in Frannie's head. It was so full of dreams. I know that I disappointed her. She was hoping for Prince Charming, and what she got was me."

12
Trouble

Honk! Honk!

The driver of a car that had been caught behind the caravan for miles was losing his patience. He'd sounded his horn several times to let them know his opinion of their slow pace. Unfortunately, the road was not much wider than a track and there was no room to pull over. Still, the driver tried numerous times to pass.

"There's a wide place up ahead, Papa, on the left," Ivy said, pointing.

Unwilling to wait a minute longer, the driver suddenly swerved out and around them, clipping the side of the two-wheeled cart. He sped away in an angry cloud of dust, without stopping to see what damage he might have inflicted.

Almost immediately there was an ominous scraping sound, and Dora began to struggle with the load. "Whoa, girl!" Alva cried. He and Ivy jumped down from the wagon to investigate.

To their horror, they discovered that the car with its impatient driver had broken the wheel on the left side of the cart. The cart had dropped onto its axle, causing it to dig deeply into the gravel and spill its contents onto the road. Loose shoes and broken packages lay in the dust.

Without wasting any time, Alva unhooked the cart, and Ivy led Dora and the caravan safely off the road on the other side.

His face ashen, Alva stood back and surveyed the damage. There was a spare wheel for the caravan, tied up underneath it, but there was nothing to replace the smaller wheel of the cart.

Together they dragged the crippled vehicle into the long grass, and both worked feverishly to clear the road of shoes. Luckily, only one other car came along, and he gave them a wide berth.

"Now what, Papa?" Ivy asked.

Alva combed his fingers through his damp hair before picking his hat up from the road. "I think we'd best carry on to the next farm," he said. "See if we can find someone there to help me fix the wheel."

Ivy offered to wait right there, guarding the loose contents of the cart, but her father wouldn't hear of it. Before they could go for help, they had to load all the shoes and the pieces of the shattered wheel into the caravan.

There were few houses on this road, and when at last they turned in at a farm gate, Ivy caught sight through the trees of a barn with a collapsed roof. "I don't think anyone lives here anymore, Papa," she said.

The lane was so narrow that they were forced to keep going until they reached the end, branches scraping the sides of the caravan all the way along.

Ivy's heart sank even further when the house appeared, its front door hanging open above a crumbling stoop. Birds darted out through broken windows at their approach.

She climbed down to look for a place wide enough for Alva to turn the wagon around. It took three tries before Dora and the caravan were facing back the way they'd come. Ivy tried not to think how late they were going to be for the fair.

Looking back over her shoulder as they rolled away, she wondered what might have befallen the family that had abandoned the house. Were they victims of the hard times her grandmother spoke of so often?

They were still several miles from the town of Birch Hills when they saw a farm wagon, drawn by a pair of chestnut horses, coming toward them, a man and woman sitting at the front. Drawing nearer, Ivy saw that the wagon carried crates and boxes that served as seats for several young children.

"This is the way to the Travellers' Fair, isn't it?" Alva called out. The wagon came alongside, and the other driver halted his team.

"We haven't seen a sign for Birch Hills since we cut off onto this road yesterday," Alva said. "We're headed to the Travellers' Fair. I know we're late, but we ran into some trouble."

"Well, you missed it," the other man declared.

"It's over?"

"Not exactly." All the occupants of the other wagon began to talk at once.

"There is no fair."

"We all got turned away."

"They made us pack up and go."

"We were the last ones to leave," the driver said, "'cos one of the youngsters was real sick." His wife was holding on her lap a small child with flaming red cheeks. As if on cue, the child gave a harsh cough and buried its face against the woman's breast.

"What happened?" Alva asked.

"Seems after last year, the shopkeepers in town had a meeting," the man said. "Decided travellers weren't welcome anymore. Claimed they were taking business away from the stores in Birch Hills.

"So, we all get there last evening — and there's fewer of us every year now — and we all start to set up. Then, this here delegation shows up and tells us we've got to move on. The people carried signs and there was a lot of angry words spoke.

"The littlest girl here was feeling poorly, so they let us stay till this morning when the druggist opened up for us, so's we could get her some medicine."

"This is real bad news," Alva said. "But suppose we've got something they don't sell in town?"

The man shook his head. "Don't seem to matter. We've got some real nice yard goods in our wagon. Straight from the cotton mill in Ridgeland. I bet there's a few in that town who can afford something better than flour-sack 'lengeree' — but they're not about to buy it from us."

"I'm real sorry about that." Alva shot Ivy a glance. "Ivy here was looking forward to the fair. Heck, so was I, if the truth be told."

"We've got shoes," Ivy said, brightly. "All kinds and sizes."

"Well, they don't want 'em." And with that, the

driver clucked at his horses, and they headed away down the road, the children on the back waving forlornly at Ivy.

"Do you think any of those kids are wearing underwear made out of flour sacks?" she asked, when they were alone again on the road.

"If they're lucky," Alva said. "These are not easy times, Ivy. Some folks say what we're going through now is what's called a depression. It could be it's only going to get worse."

"But we don't have to go back, do we, Papa?"

"No, we don't," Alva said. "I still have to see if I can find someone to fix that cart wheel. — *Gee up, Dora!* — I think I'd like to have a look at this place called Birch Hills."

13
Birch Hills

On the high ground that overlooked the village, Ivy and Alva passed an open field where the grass had been trampled. A Union Jack was flapping in the breeze. A banner, held to a tree by one remaining cord, lay draped over the ground.

"Go home." Alva read one of the hand-painted signs attached to wooden stakes stuck in the grass near the entrance to the campground.

"*Peddlers*, go home," said Ivy. "That means us, Papa. Maybe this isn't such a good idea."

At the top of the main street of Birch Hills, above all the shops, they pulled up at a feed mill, a barn-like structure with a pull-through for wagons. "It'll be fine, Ivy," Alva said. "We aren't here to try to sell the folks anything. I'm just going to talk to the boys in here. See if they know where's the best place to get a wheel fixed."

He swung down from the wagon, and Ivy sat and surveyed the town below. It looked friendly enough. The shops on the main street were just opening for the day's business, and there were few people out and about. A couple of youths on bicycles rode past, craning their necks to see who the strangers with the caravan might be.

Ivy watched a shopkeeper down the street come out to sweep the sidewalk in front of his establishment. Another appeared and began turning a crank which lowered an awning over his shop window. They both took long looks up the hill toward the wagon. Together they crossed the street and went into a store on the other side.

After the men came back out, a small group of people began to gather. There was much gesturing toward the caravan. Ivy's heart began to beat faster.

She hoped they were just curious, but when they started moving together up the hill in her direction, talking amongst themselves and collecting more supporters as they advanced, Ivy knew they had something on their minds. She gave an involuntary shiver.

The citizens stopped in front of Dora. One of the men stepped out of the group and walked right up to where Ivy sat.

"She's just a kid," he said, with some surprise, to the others.

Ivy cast an anxious glance at the door of the feed mill, willing her father to appear.

"The man who was with her went inside," someone in the crowd called out.

"You folks peddlers?" It was the spokesman.

"We came about a broken wheel," Ivy said. "My father will be back in a minute."

"But you're peddlers," he said.

"We're travellers," Ivy said. "My father is a shoe salesman."

The man sneered. "Forget the fancy talk. Whatever you call yourselves, you're not welcome here. We thought we'd cleared all you people out."

Suddenly, a boy at the far edge of the crowd picked up a small stone and threw it in the direction of the caravan. It struck Dora on the left flank, startling her, and she moved forward — not very far — but far enough that a few people who'd crowded too close thought they were in danger of being trampled. The tone of their voices turned angry.

Ivy snatched up the reins. "Whoa, Dora!"

The obedient creature had already stopped, but Ivy could see her ears twitch in agitation. Ivy gave the crowd of unfriendly citizens the fiercest glare she could muster, though her heart was hammering in her ears.

All at once, Alva was there, walking around in front of Dora, patting her neck and saying something to calm her.

"Well, folks, I can tell this here's no welcoming committee," he said. He pushed his way through the cluster around his caravan.

"We made it plain, mister," the spokesman said. "We want no peddlers in Birch Hills. It's hard enough to keep our shops going, without you people coming in and stealing our customers."

"I steal from no one, sir," Alva said evenly. He climbed up onto the wagon and sat down, taking the reins from Ivy. "Good day to you, then."

The crowd shifted a little to let them through.

"I think you are the rudest people I have *ever* met in my *entire* life!" Ivy said in a loud voice. "I'd never set foot in this miserable town for all the tea in China."

She was the only one who heard Alva's warning, "Ivy. That's enough now."

They moved off with what Ivy considered was great dignity, although it was hard to maintain when they had to circle at the bottom of the street and pass the jeering crowd once more, on the way out of town.

Still, Alva and Ivy both managed to keep their spines stiff and their eyes straight ahead.

"That's that, I guess," was all Alva had to say, as they passed again the deserted campground. "I got no help from the folks at the feed mill neither."

"We didn't do anything to make those people treat us like that," Ivy said. Even when she and Frannie had endured the wrath of their landlords because the rent was overdue, she'd known the anger had been justified. "They hated us, Papa. For no reason."

"Don't take it personally, Ivy."

"But it was personal. I was the one sitting there when they came up the hill, looking like they wanted to tear someone to pieces."

"Those folks were just het up at travellers in general," her father said. "You heard what the man with the sick child said this morning. The townspeople are afraid the travellers are going to take away their livelihoods. It's natural they'd want to protect that."

"They could have tried to find a better way to do it."

"You'd think so," Alva agreed. "But that's what happens sometimes when a crowd gets going. All it takes is one or two hotheads, and if the rest are followers, things can get ugly. First thing you know, you've got yourselves a mob. And common sense goes out the window."

"You've seen that happen, Papa?"

"Saw it with my own eyes, at one of the mines up north. Bunch of fools, upset at the boss, let themselves get talked into tearing down the pit head, with their bare hands."

"If you hadn't come along when you did, Papa," Ivy said, "I can just imagine what they'd have done to me."

"Well, I *did* come along," Alva said. "And that's the end of it. It's not like you, Ivy, to think of the worst thing that could happen."

Alva had nothing more to say on the subject.

At midday, they stopped for lunch in a grove of trees and ate a few of the ripe tomatoes they'd bought from a farm stand along the road that morning. Ivy spent the rest of the afternoon bent over her book, pencil in hand. Writing didn't help her to understand the humiliation she'd suffered, but after she had recorded the event in her book, she did feel better. It was as if, once written, she didn't have to think of it again.

Toward evening they passed their cart, lying like a wounded creature in the grass at the side of the road. They stopped only long enough to leave off the broken pieces of the wheel.

"Anyone who wants it is welcome to it," Alva said, and he dusted off his hands.

Ivy felt compelled to imagine a happier ending for the little cart, to keep her heart from breaking at the idea of abandoning it.

"Maybe whoever finds it will be a person who really needs it, Papa. That person will fix it up and suddenly, having a little cart like that will make the most wonderful difference in his life."

"Now that sounds more like the Ivy Chalmers I know."

She would try not to disappoint him again.

14
The Birthday Present

"It's time that I admit it," Alva said, stirring the campfire with a stick of kindling one evening. "The days of the salesman who travels by horse and wagon are over."

"Don't say that," Ivy begged. "Please, Papa." But she'd watched with an aching heart as her father struggled to keep from breaking into a run earlier that day as a man chased him off his property. Sales had not gotten any better after the ugly incident in Birch Hills.

"It's the truth, Ivy," Alva said. "It's looking us right in the eye. Now that more folks have cars, they can drive into town and shop for themselves. Don't need to wait for the traveller to call."

The light from the fire cast deep valleys of shadow on Alva's face. Ivy had noticed lately how loosely his clothes seemed to hang on his lean body. She knew how tired he must be, and she had begun to worry about his health.

"So what do you want to do then, Papa?" she asked. "Summer's not even over yet." She made up her mind that she would accept whatever decision he made about the rest of the journey.

"Pretty near over," Alva said. "I think we'd best take the shortest route home now. Get you back to your grandmother's before the end of August."

It was the last thing Ivy wanted to hear. She felt like a deflated balloon. Hugging her knees to her chest, she hid her face from him.

"Your grandmother will want to help you get ready for school, child," Alva said, his voice soft. "What grade will you be going in?"

"I don't know," Ivy said. "Junior Fourth, I guess. I don't always go to school."

"Ivy, look at me. Why not?"

She raised her head and gave a shrug. "Because Momma and I have to move sometimes. I just get started at one school, and then we're off again to a new place. Anyway, school seems like a waste of time to me. I can learn more out of the books I get at the library."

"School's important, Ivy. Take that from someone who didn't get enough of it."

"Well, Grandmother told me that these days even lawyers are selling brushes door-to-door."

"Likely true enough." Alva tossed the stick into the fire, causing a shower of sparks.

"What I really want to do is write, Papa," Ivy said, with passion. "I want to be a writer. I have stories in my head just bursting to get out."

"Pretty sure a writer needs to go to school," said Alva.

The cicadas rattled from sun-up to dark on the hottest days, and the dust rose with every clop of Dora's hooves. Every stream or swimming hole they passed was an invitation to Ivy.

On the day of Ivy's thirteenth birthday, just as they passed a signpost indicating that they were two miles from the village of Hammond, she caught a glimpse of sunlight on water, glittering like silver between the trees.

"This would be a perfect place to spend the night, Papa."

They had learned, after Birch Hills, not to try making any sales in town, and this was far enough away from Hammond that no one would try to run them off.

"I think there's a lake down there," Ivy said. "Come on, Papa. Let's have a swim."

"It's only two o'clock," Alva said, but he pulled back on the reins anyway. "Well, seeing as this is a special day," he said. "You can have a swim while I take stock of the inventory."

Dora drew the caravan into the trees above the lake. "But it's way too hot inside, Papa, to count shoes," Ivy pointed out.

Alva was forced to agree. He lifted the back window of the caravan to try to coax a breeze through, and he and Ivy went down to the water together.

Before them lay a small lake with a beach of smooth stones. "Looks pretty safe, but let me go first." Alva pulled off his boots and waded out, splashing water over his face and forearms.

"Doesn't drop off too quick. You can go ahead," he said, returning to shore. "No farther than your waist, mind. Think I'll just go up and sit for a spell. I'm feeling a little tired."

Ivy gave him a close look. "Are you all right, Papa? We can count the stock together, after it cools off. I'll help you. Promise me you won't try to do it now."

"I'll have no trouble keeping that promise," he said, with a wry smile. "But you won't mind if I stretch out in the shade, will you?"

"No, Papa. You should go up and rest."

Ivy waded into the water till she was waist deep. It was deliciously cool and she ducked down, forcing her dress under the water, spreading her arms and twirling about.

Only once had she ever owned a bathing suit, one childhood summer when she'd been given a hand-me-down in a deep shade of red. The colour had bled into the white piping around the neck and legs, turning it pink.

She'd worn that scratchy bathing suit proudly whenever she and Frannie went with Gloria to Cherry Beach, happy not to have to strip down to her cotton bloomers that summer.

She had never learned to swim well, but could hold her breath and open her eyes underwater. She used to try catching the minnows that darted through her fingers, or to pick up pretty stones off the bottom to show to Frannie, who sat on the crowded sand, fanning herself and chatting with Gloria.

Ivy turned toward shore, that memory so vivid in her mind that she half expected to see the two young women lounging there. But where was Papa?

When Alva still hadn't come down after what seemed like a very long time, Ivy decided that he must indeed have fallen asleep. She lingered on the beach until curiosity got the better of her, and she climbed the bank to the caravan.

There was no sign of her father. She looked inside

the wagon, but he wasn't there. He had unhitched Dora and filled the horse's tub with water from the icebox, but now he was nowhere in sight.

Where would he have gone, after telling her he was so tired?

Ivy looked back down the road in the direction they had come. She started walking, scanning the road through the shimmer of heat and checking over her shoulder every few seconds, unsure which way he'd gone. Her dress dried quickly in the blazing sun.

Finally, she saw Alva coming toward her.

"Did you think you'd lost me?" he teased, when he reached her side and saw the look of relief on her face. He was wearing an uncharacteristic grin. "Happy birthday, Ivy," he said.

Before she could say anything, Alva held out his hands, and Ivy saw that he was holding a tiny kitten. Its coat was the most unusual shade of bluish grey, and its eyes were the colour of the August sky. The soft creature looked out of place in those rough hands.

Ivy took the kitten from him gently and held it against her neck. "Oh, Papa, is it really for me?"

"Of course. Do you see anyone else around here having a birthday?"

He drew a jar of milk from of his trouser pocket.

"This will do till we get to Hammond," he said. "We need another chunk of ice anyway."

"I read what it said on a sign by the road, a ways back," Alva explained, hitching Dora up to the wagon again. "'Free kittens.' Thought you might've seen it, too. But I guess you were too busy looking for a place to swim."

"But you saw it, Papa, and you knew what it said, too! Didn't I tell you that you could learn to read?"

Alva steadied her as she climbed back up onto the wagon and handed her the kitten when she was settled. "That you did, Ivy," he said. "That you did."

❧

By the time they arrived at their camp for the night, on the far side of the village, Ivy had come up with a perfect name for the kitten. "I used to pretend that grandmother's place on Arthur Road was Camelot, so I'm going to call her Guinevere. Isn't that the most beautiful name? Guinevere was Arthur's queen."

Alva frowned. "Is that a boy's name? It's a male cat, you know."

"Oh, is it? Well, that's all right. I'll just call him Merlin." And Ivy proceeded to tell her father the part the magician had played in the legend of King Arthur.

The August evening was chilly, and they sat close to the fire after supper that night. Merlin was snug inside the front of Ivy's old green sweater. She had already introduced him to Dora, holding the mewing ball of fur up to the horse's nose.

Ivy watched the sparks from the fire fly upward and disappear into the dark. "I certainly didn't expect you to give me a birthday present, Papa." It pleased her to see the happiness in Alva's face.

With the end of her travels with her father in sight, Ivy's thoughts turned more and more to Frannie. Would she have come to Maud's place while they were away?

Part of her hoped that Frannie would already be waiting for her at Maud's, proving to her grandmother that her mother had not deserted her.

Ivy had dreamed one night that she was looking for her mother, searching the empty nighttime streets, the filthy alleys behind the tenements. The dream had seemed so real that Ivy thought, even on waking, that she'd heard her mother's voice tell her not to try to find her. But it was only a dream, and Ivy knew that if Frannie had already come to Larkin, she would not go home without her. She would be waiting.

If she hadn't come yet, at the very least there would be lots of letters for Ivy at 54 Arthur Road, news of Frannie and when they could go home together.

Where her father was concerned, Ivy was determined not to lose him again. "Let's make a pact, Papa," she said, hearing him come in to his bed at the back of the caravan that night. "Let's agree to keep in touch always. After you drop me off and take the caravan back to the shoe factory, I know you'll be looking for work. But promise me you and I will spend time together, once we're all back in Toronto."

"Whenever we can," Alva said. Ivy heard him groan as he settled his bones on the narrow bench. "That I can promise, child."

15

The Journey Ends

Two days out of Larkin it began to rain. Ivy and her father hadn't seen much rain that summer, only showers that came and went within a few minutes, leaving rainbows in a sky so wide that, for the first time in her life, Ivy got to see both the beginning and the end.

It seemed to her now as if all of nature was sighing with relief over the gift of rain — the trees grown heavy with summer, the parched fields, even the grey weeds that struggled for a place at the edge of the road.

"Isn't it wonderful, Papa?" Ivy stood and held her face and arms up to the rain, and Alva, laughing out loud, tossed his dust-covered hat over his shoulder into the wagon.

The rain continued without let-up for the rest of the journey. Water slid off Dora's back in sheets and pounded on the roof of the caravan till Ivy couldn't hear her own voice.

Alva, who had to sit out on the seat in order to drive, was often soaked through, in spite of the rain cape Ivy hung over his shoulders. She felt guilty about staying warm and dry inside with her kitten and wished she could trade places with him.

They had cleared the shoe boxes from around the little stove in the caravan when the rain began, and Alva had lit it for the first time that night, to cook their supper and to dry his clothing.

⮜⮞

It was still raining when they pulled up in front of the narrow grey house on Arthur Road. To Ivy, peering hopefully out over Alva's shoulder, the place looked the same as it had when they'd left. There was nothing to indicate that her mother might be inside.

"Come on then, Ivy." Alva raised the cape over his head and drew her under its shelter.

There was no sense waiting for the rain to let up. They made a run for the house, throwing open the gate, splashing through the puddles, and leaping onto the front porch.

Maud appeared inside the screen door. "My good

heavens!" she said. "Just look at the pair of you. A couple of drowned rats, if ever I saw one."

"Have you ever, Grandmother?" Ivy said, gasping. "Seen a drowned rat? I have and it's horrible. It had fallen into the rain barrel, in the alley behind the diner. It was all swoll up and ..."

"I see the girl hasn't managed to talk herself out yet," Maud said, holding the door with one out-stretched arm for the dripping pair to enter.

"I guess Mama's not here yet," Ivy said when Maud insisted she go upstairs without another word and put on some dry clothing. "I'll be back down to get my mail."

Hurrying downstairs again, Ivy found her father and grandmother in the kitchen. "How many letters did I get while I was away?" she asked eagerly.

Maud was spreading Alva's suit jacket on a rack behind the stove. "Not a single one, I'm afraid."

"Grandmother, please don't tease me. I've read Momma's first letter so many times that the folds wore through. There must be more."

"Guess your mother's so busy in New York she doesn't have time to write letters," Alva said. "Could be she's in lots and lots of those plays by now."

Ivy sank onto one of the chairs at the table. It couldn't be true. "But that would mean she won't be back for ages," she said. "Why did she have to go so far away to become a star?"

"We'll worry about that later, Ivy," Maud said. "For now, I've got a real nice pot of soup made here, and your father's going to have a bite to eat."

She set a steaming bowl on the table in front of Ivy and handed her a spoon. "Eat," she said. "If there's a little left you can feed it to that cat of yours. Though no one ever thought to ask me if I wanted a cat in the house."

Ivy bent her face over the bowl, closing her eyes to keep in the tears, inhaling the fragrance of vegetables and broth.

As soon as Alva had eaten, he set off down the street to see if one of the local merchants would take the shoes from his paid-up stock off his hands. He would be leaving in the morning.

Ivy was drying the supper dishes when Maud unexpectedly turned from the sink and left the room. When she returned, she handed Ivy the envelope from Frannie's one and only letter.

Ivy frowned. "What's this? You said there were no …"

"It's from the first letter. Something you need to see," Maud said. "Did you have a good look at that postmark when you got it?"

"I don't remember." Ivy set the tea towel aside.

Now that was strange. Frannie's envelope bore a Canadian stamp — a two-cent Canadian stamp. The name of the postal station where it had been mailed was smudged and almost illegible, but "Ontario, Canada," was as plain as could be.

"I don't understand," Ivy said.

"Your mother's letter didn't come from New York at all, Ivy. It was mailed somewhere here in Ontario."

"It couldn't have been. Why wouldn't I have seen that before?"

"Well, it was the letter you were most interested in," Maud said. "You left the envelope here on the table, and I put it in with the scrap paper. When I was tidying things after you and Alva left, I found it again."

"I don't understand how Momma's letter could have come from Ontario. How could that be possible?"

"I've had all summer to ask myself the same question," Maud said. "Maybe Frannie never went to New York City in the first place."

"I don't believe that! Of course she went. Someone else must have brought the letter back here to mail. That's it! Maybe Gloria went to visit, and Momma gave her the letter to mail when she got home."

"That could have happened," Maud said.

"I'm sure that's the way it was. It makes perfect sense to me." And before her grandmother could suggest otherwise, Ivy hung up the towel and left the room. "I'm going out to say hello to my chickens."

"You can let them out into the yard," Maud said, before the door closed between them, "now that it's stopped raining."

Swinging open the wire gate on the chicken coop, Ivy greeted each of the ten hens by name, relieved that her grandmother had not murdered any of them while she'd been away.

She stood back and watched the hens walk their peculiar walk — pecking and scratching, bobbing and nodding — down the rows of the now depleted garden.

Ivy was up early the next morning, so that she could spend the last few minutes with her father. She sat memorizing the lines in his face while he ate his breakfast.

"Remember to keep practising your reading, Papa," Ivy said. "You don't need to wait till you've got a book to read. You have to read everything — road signs, notices, everything." Lifting a familiar red package from beside the stove, she set it in front of him.

"Red River Cereal," Alva read. "Contains wheat, rye, and flax."

Out on the front porch, Ivy bade him a tearful farewell, wringing more promises from him that the minute he found a place to live, he'd let her know. And because Maud, too, was depending on him, Ivy trusted that he would keep in touch.

"You are my one bright light, Ivy," Alva said from the bottom step.

"I made you happy, didn't I, Papa?"

"Indeed you did, child. Happier'n I've been in a long while."

❧❧

With Alva gone, Ivy had to face the other possible explanation for the Ontario postmark on Frannie's letter. Had her mother been playing her old game of "let's pretend" when she wrote to say that she was enjoying life in New York City? Is that what Maud had also been thinking? That she'd been in Ontario all along?

"You can live wherever you want to," Frannie used to say. "You are the one who gets to decide." Every time they'd moved from one miserable rooming house to the next, she'd ask, "Where will it be this time?"

And the new place would become Shangri-La, or some other make-believe paradise for the two of them, where no hardships would ever be acknowledged.

Frannie's letter had talked about the sights of New York City, the tall buildings, the Statue of Liberty, the bustling city. But who hadn't heard of those attractions? Was Frannie ever even there?

So many questions. All she knew for sure was that her mother had gone *somewhere* ... somewhere away from her only daughter. And it was up to Ivy to find her.

If anyone had any news of Frannie it would be Gloria Klein. Gloria had never had a telephone, but neither had Maud. Ivy sat down at once and wrote a letter to her mother's best friend. She didn't know the number of Gloria's building, but how many Gloria Kleins could there be on Coxwell Avenue in Toronto?

The letter came back by return mail, stamped "Unknown."

"Of course, she's not unknown!" Ivy was indignant. "Lots of people know Gloria. Why didn't they just ask someone? All her customers at the diner adore her.

"That's it: The diner! Oh, what was it called? It was right there, on the corner." She slapped her forehead, looking helplessly at her grandmother. "Was it Maxie's? Or Manny's?"

"One time, years ago, I ate at a place in Toronto called McNeilly's," Maud said.

"No, too many letters," Ivy said, counting them on her fingers. "Half the lights on the sign were burnt out, and no one ever replaced them. I don't think I ever knew for sure what the place was called. We just called it Gloria's diner."

"It'll come to you," Maud said. "And you will kindly keep that cat of yours off the table."

Ivy tucked Merlin under her arm. "He's just a kitten, Grandmother." But if he was ever going to get along with her grandmother, Ivy was going to have to teach Merlin some manners.

It was another name that popped into Ivy's head in the middle of the night: Johnny Dracup. Dracup's Bake Shop on Queen Street. She'd write to Johnny.

Ivy was sure that the man would remember her mother. She had sometimes suspected that Johnny had been sweet on Frannie. There was a good chance that he had heard some news of her.

"Dear Mr. Dracup," the letter began. "My name is Ivy Chalmers …"

PART TWO

Charlie

16
Charlie's Story

The 1930s were no easier on the country's farmers than on anyone else, but Rena Bayliss and her teen-aged nephew, Charlie, residents of the third concession north of Larkin, were used to "making do."

Rena and her aging father, Garnet, had sold off most of the family farm back in 1928 when Charlie was twelve, keeping the larger of the two houses on the property and three acres of land. Besides raising chickens, Rena grew all her own vegetables, earned a meagre wage at the canning factory in season, and took in sewing.

Charlie's mother had died when he was still an infant, leaving him with no memory of her at all. The only thing the boy owned that had once belonged to his mother was a silver hand mirror.

He had been just four when he discovered the mirror in one of the drawers in his aunt's sewing machine.

"What does it say on the back?" he had asked.

Rena removed her feet from the treadle of the machine and read to him the words engraved in the tarnished silver. "It says, 'To Dottie. Forever, Alva.' You should have that mirror, Charlie," she said solemnly. "It belonged to your mother."

It was much later when Charlie learned that, although his mother had been married to the man who'd given her the mirror, he was not Charlie's father.

Charlie never met his real father. He'd gone away to fight in the Great War and had died in a muddy field somewhere in France, outside a town whose name Charlie couldn't even pronounce.

Now past sixty, and her coronet of braids completely white, Rena Bayliss had never married, but had always considered Charlie her own.

"You were *our* baby, born right here in this house," she used to tell the little boy, who sat on the floor beside her, building tractors and wagons with bits of cardboard and empty spools of thread, while she did alterations for her customers.

"Oh, your grandparents and I were heartbroken all right, when the two of you went off to live with Dottie's new husband in the city. But Dottie was happy, and she'd married a kind man. Your poor mother, God rest her soul, got sick and died within the year. And so we got you back again."

Rena would squint at the cloth her fingers were guiding under the needle, her feet rocking the treadle while she spoke.

"We lost track of the man after that, but I do remember his grief at losing Dottie. He knew you belonged with us, though, and he went back to Toronto alone. Climbed right back into the hearse that had brought you and your mother home.

"We saw him just one more time after that. A friend had driven him and his new bride over to Larkin to meet his mother. While they were there, he came out to the farm, wanting to see you. He was real disappointed that you didn't remember him.

"He told us then that he had remarried. I didn't get to meet the woman, though. She stayed outside in the car."

❧❧

All day an easterly wind had whipped snow into drifts across the yard behind the Bayliss house. Now, at five o'clock, it was so cold out there that Charlie thought the bottom might fall out of the thermometer on the tin Shell sign nailed to the side of the barn. His feet felt like two blocks of ice, but still Charlie delayed entering the house. Twice Aunt Rena had come to the back door to call him in for supper.

When he could stand the cold no longer, he knocked the snow off the metal shovel and set it inside the back kitchen. "All done, Aunt Rena," he said, seeing her there. "I took those ashes out and cleared the path to the outhouse again. Anything else I can help you with?"

"I don't know what's got into you, Charlie," Rena said. "I never saw you work so hard at your chores as you have this winter."

The boy reached over his aunt's head for the bottle of preserved plums she'd come for, and handed it down to her.

Rena entered the warm kitchen ahead of him. "All that wood chopped and stacked," she marvelled. "My land, it's like someone lit a fire under you."

Miss Taylor, the schoolteacher who boarded with them, had already taken her seat at the supper table. "Charlie's very helpful in the classroom, too," she said, as if he wasn't standing right behind her, washing up under the pump at the kitchen sink. "He's the first one on his feet to put wood in the stove or to fill the gasoline lamps."

Charlie felt his face turn as red as his hair. The other boys in school teased him mercilessly about the pretty, young boarder, shouldering him off the road into the snowbanks on the way home, hooting with laughter.

"Ah, you're all just jealous," Charlie would shout, scooping up handfuls of snow and pelting them with snowballs. They could poke fun at him all they liked. Charlie knew something they didn't: Miss Taylor was engaged to be married. She'd be gone as soon as school was out for the summer.

Charlie Bayliss's favourite pastime on warm summer evenings was playing softball with the other boys from the area. Charlie could connect with the ball with such force that he'd hit it way out past left field, or take everyone by surprise with a mean line drive.

"Tighten up, guys," the other team would yell, whenever Charlie made a hit that got him on base. They were all familiar with the way Charlie would dance on and off the bases, teasing the pitcher into throwing the ball, so that Charlie could attempt one of his spectacular slides into home plate.

The players had organized themselves into two teams, the "Farmers" and the "Townies." Charlie was a Farmer, and his friend Delbert Coon, the fair-haired, raw-boned youth whose father owned a grocery store on the main street in Larkin, was a Townie.

The boys could always count on someone bringing a softball to the game, and they'd share any gloves that could be found. But you couldn't play serious baseball in bare feet, and Charlie had already worn out his only pair of shoes.

Aunt Rena had found him an old pair of Grandpa's boots to wear. The left one had a piece of corrugated cardboard tucked down inside to cover a hole in the sole.

"They'll have to do, Charlie," Rena said, "till you can save up enough money to buy yourself a proper pair of running shoes."

Just in time, Edwin Fennell, the man who'd bought the Bayliss property, came around to Rena's back door, asking to hire Charlie.

"I've got myself a contract to grow peas this summer." The big man leaned against the door frame. "Ten acres of 'em, for the canners in Larkin. I sure could use your help, Charlie. I'll pay you, too, of course."

That's the part Charlie was waiting for.

It turned out to be a very good year for peas. When the crop was ready to harvest, Edwin Fennell rode the horse that pulled the pea rake along the rows. It was Charlie's job to pitch the heavy green vines up onto the steel-tired wagon.

Because the peas were so abundant, the horse could only go a short distance before the long tines of the rake were full. It would then have to be dragged off the field and the vines shaken out before they could continue. It was slow, tedious work in the hot sun.

By the time Charlie drove the wagon to the factory, there was often a wait of several hours to get it unloaded. Sitting on the wagon seat under the blazing sun, watching Fennell's pair of horses flick flies off their backsides, Charlie decided there must be an easier way to make a living than farming.

Mr. Fennell's five-acre field of tomatoes, where Charlie and Aunt Rena, with the energy of someone half her age, had laboured as pickers, netted the farmer only forty-five dollars. No one wanted to buy his oats, even at twenty cents a bushel. Where had the good years gone?

When the season was over, Mr. Fennell told them that it was the five hundred dollars he got for his crop of peas that meant the difference between bankruptcy and being able to hang on to the old Bayliss farm.

That made Charlie feel a little better. "But, by George," he said to his friend Delbert, "when next summer rolls around, I'll find myself another way to make some money."

17
Mr. Matthie

The new schoolteacher arrived in September. Mr. Matthie was tall and balding, with a pencil-thin moustache. His coat hung on his thin frame like the clothes on a scarecrow.

There weren't too many of Charlie's old pals left in school now. They were needed to help support their families and had gotten certificates that permitted them to quit school before their sixteenth birthdays.

When Charlie suggested he do the same, Rena encouraged him to stay in school. "Sure, we could use a little more money," she said. "But you go to school as long as we can manage here. Least till you write your high school entrance."

For now, the barter system served them well. Rena's mustard pickles or a few jars of her pumpkin preserves could be traded for some meat for the table, or the occasional bag of coal for the Quebec heater in the front room.

For a lady's coat she'd cut down and remade to fit a child, Rena was able to get some patching done on the roof of the house, and if Charlie did odd jobs for the neighbours, he would often be paid in plums or apples.

When Mr. Matthie came around to the house, hoping to board with them as the previous teacher had, Aunt Rena quickly agreed.

Garnet Bayliss had slipped away in his sleep the July just passed, but there should be no tongues wagging over Mr. Matthie living at Rena's. Charlie was the man of the house now, and at fourteen he was tall and well muscled after his summer on the farm.

Although Mr. Matthie didn't smell half as good as Miss Taylor had, the man loved to go fishing, and that made him all right in Charlie's mind.

But when the ice melted the following spring, and Charlie could have been spearing pike in the Pechart River with the other boys, Mr. Matthie was right there in the Bayliss kitchen, making sure that Charlie did his homework every night.

"I'm counting on you to pass that entrance examination," the teacher said. "You don't want to end up peeling tomatoes at the canning factory for the rest of your life."

Late in May, the local priest made a call to the Bayliss home. None of the Baylisses had been church-goers, but that didn't stop the priest from calling around. The coins on the collection plate at the church of St. Basil's-on-the-Corner were getting a little sparse these days.

The priest had ridden his bicycle out to the farm, and his cassock and black hat were coated in dust. After a cold drink in Rena's kitchen, she'd led him outside, into the shade of the elms that grew between the house and the barn where Charlie was chopping wood.

"It's good to see a strong young man helping his auntie," remarked the priest. "I have a regular parish-ioner in town who could use a hand once in a while. If you are willing, young man."

Charlie rested on the ax handle and listened.

"The lady probably won't be able to pay much, but you'd be doing a real good deed. She lives all alone and is too proud to ask for help. What do you say?"

It was Rena who spoke up first. "I could spare the boy for part of a day," she said. "And whatever the lady cares to give him, in exchange for his time, will come in handy."

"I'll tell her to expect the lad," said the priest. "Hers is the only house with a picket fence around it on Arthur Road. You know the street next to the tracks?"

Charlie assured him that he did. But after walking the five miles into town the next day, Charlie discovered that what the lady of the house wanted was for him to shovel chicken manure. As if he didn't have enough of that to do at home.

Her weekly cleaning of the henhouse over the winter had resulted in a large pile of dung, and now that the weather was warm, it had to be moved to the farthest corner of her yard.

When he was finally finished the job, and hot and stinking of chicken manure, Charlie was handed a box of soda biscuits for his labour. He had no money to pay for a cold drink at Coon's as he'd hoped, so he just headed home instead, stopping off for his first swim of the season in the Pechart River.

Although the ice had been out of Misty Lake — the source of the Pechart — for a month, the waters of the river, flowing swiftly south and passing through Larkin on the way to Lake Ontario, were still frigid.

Charlie left his cap and boots onshore and waded out in his overalls. He forced himself to swim upstream against the current until his arms and legs grew tired.

Then he let the river carry him back to the place where he'd entered the water.

He had climbed up the riverbank and was cutting through the ditch to get to the road again, when he spotted a man swinging a golf club through the long grass. A large house rose above the bushes on the left.

"Hey, sonny." The man was talking to him. "Did you see a golf ball down in there?"

"Wasn't really looking," Charlie said.

The man, who was short and round in the middle, was dressed for a game of golf, wearing plaid socks that met the bottom of a pair of knickers — Mr. Matthie had called them "plus-fours."

"I'll go have a look," Charlie said, and he slid down to the ditch again.

"Mind yourself," the man said. "That looks like poison ivy in there."

"Oh, I had poison ivy once," Charlie said, choosing to forget the miserable days he'd spent spotted with clumps of dried baking soda. "It was nothing, just a bit of an itch." He held up a white ball. "Is this it?"

"Why, thank you, son. Say, you wouldn't happen to be looking for a job, would you?"

"Sure. Who isn't?"

"They can always use caddies over at the Shady Dell Golf Club. It's where I play on Saturdays. Drop by sometime, if you're interested in making a little extra cash." The man reached out to shake Charlie's hand. "Name's Harry Pike."

Only a few businessmen from the area could afford to play golf at Shady Dell during the thirties. It was doubtful that the club could have survived without the wealthy men from Toronto driving out for a day on the links.

The town had converted some vacant land into a municipal golf course, on the other side of the river. You could play all day there for fifty cents, carrying your own mid-iron and putter.

Charlie had no idea what a caddy did to earn his pay, but by the time he got home and remembered that he'd left the box of soda biscuits on the riverbank, he'd decided that caddying was likely much better than cleaning henhouses.

❧

The day before school got out for the summer, Charlie took their boarder fishing for the last time. Mr. Matthie would be going home in a few days, and in September he'd be teaching at a school over in Dillfield.

The fishing was good in Misty Lake, over on the next concession. So good, in fact, that, using a couple of Charlie's spinners with worms attached, he and Mr. Matthie could go out late in the afternoon and, within a half-hour of casting out, catch enough pickerel for the supper table.

Charlie guided the little flat-bottomed boat that he kept hidden in the bushes, down the grassy slope to the water. Grabbing the rope on the bow, he pulled the vessel back to the shore so that Mr. Matthie could board.

"Step right into the middle there, sir," Charlie said.

"If you hate farming, Charlie, as much as you say you do." The teacher had picked up his favourite topic of conversation again. "You really should continue your education, broaden your horizons."

Charlie wished that Mr. Matthie wouldn't use these fishing expeditions as opportunities to lecture him about staying in school. He had passed his entrance, but he wasn't sure what he should do next. In another month he'd be fifteen, and he was thinking seriously about looking for work.

"I can't go to my regular school, now that I've finished Senior Fourth," Charlie said.

He shoved the boat out, and when the water was up to his knees, clambered aboard himself. "The high school's in Larkin, you know. And that's five miles away."

"That shouldn't bother a strapping young man like you. Why don't you get yourself a bicycle? Maybe someone in the neighbourhood has a car even, and would agree to give you a lift. You just need to ask around."

"Mr. Fennell has a car," Charlie said. "A McLaughlin Buick. But he can't afford the gasoline to run it, so now it sits out in the yard behind his house. He lets me tinker with it sometimes."

"Oh, there's much to learn about automobiles, Charlie," the teacher said. "The internal combustion engine. Stay in school and learn some study skills. You'll never regret it." He passed Charlie the worm can. "These hard times will not last forever, my boy."

18
Meeting Mary Alice

"Caddy for you today, sir?" Charlie Bayliss stepped up to the car in the parking lot at the Shady Dell Golf Course. Harry Pike, owner of the Larkin Pants Factory, was unloading his clubs from the rumble seat.

"Good lad," Mr. Pike said. "Bert here yet?" The manager of the canning factory in Larkin was Mr. Pike's usual partner.

"He's waiting for you on the porch, sir. Greens are still a little damp."

"Looks like a fine day," Mr. Pike declared. "We'll get in nine holes before the sun gets too hot."

Charlie hoisted the strap on the heavy canvas bag over his shoulder and strode off toward the clubhouse.

He liked to be the first caddy to show up at the golf course on Saturday mornings. Harry Pike always came early, and Harry Pike had turned out to be the best tipper among the local golfers.

If Mr. Pike wasn't coming, Charlie hung around, hoping to be hired by some other golfer looking for a lad with a strong back to carry his bag of clubs and a keen eye for searching the rough. He wasn't often disappointed.

As soon as word got out that there was money to be made at Shady Dell, other youths from the community began to flock there to get their share of the wealth. Only the most dedicated, however, would stay on when the summer days grew long and hot, and the mosquitoes thirsted for blood in the trees along the fairways. Among this handful was young Charlie Bayliss.

With Charlie having more and more frequently to work without pay on Mr. Fennell's farm, the caddying job meant that he was still able to contribute a little money toward expenses at home. If his tips were especially generous, he might have enough left over to get into the movies in Larkin with Delbert Coon and the boys.

No sooner had he started the caddying job than Charlie learned that he could resell any unclaimed balls he found at Shady Dell over at the municipal golf course. After closing time, with the owner's blessing, he'd go searching between the trees and wading out into the pond. Even the ditches outside the golf course could yield a few stray balls from time to time.

❧

The baseball games between the Farmers and the Townies had begun to attract a loyal following of spectators, including a growing number of young ladies.

At first, it was just a handful of younger sisters of the players who tagged along, then a neighbour girl would happen by, or a visiting cousin or two. Audrey Millcroft, the eldest daughter of the town's lawyer, had her own car, and she had no trouble filling it with her friends on game nights. Before long, the boys had a regular audience of teen-aged girls cheering them on.

Some time in early August there was a new girl in the Millcroft car. Her name was Mary Alice Flint, and word was that she had her eye on the good-looking redhead, Charlie Bayliss.

Delbert Coon got a ride back into town after the game one night with Audrey and the others. While he was pretending to tease Betty Rasmussen, who sat pleasantly squeezed into the back seat beside him, he was actually listening to the chatter amongst the girls in the front, especially when his friend Charlie's name came up.

Delbert dropped by the Bayliss place on the weekend with the news. He found Charlie washing golf balls under the backyard pump. "She likes you, Charlie," Delbert said. "That Mary Alice girl. The blonde? The one who's just come to town."

"She doesn't even know me," Charlie growled.

"But she wants to meet you. She told me she did."

Seizing a golf ball, Delbert scrubbed it against the front of his shirt. "Look, I'm doing you a favour. I wish I had your way with the ladies. You just make sure you're at the game on Wednesday night because that's when I'm going to introduce you."

❧

It was Mary Alice Flint that Charlie took to the movies at the Roxy the first time he ever asked a girl out. He got a lift into Larkin with Mr. Pike, after caddying all day, and he showed up at the Coon residence right after supper. He had a clean shirt with him; one Aunt Rena had just turned the collar on.

Delbert was home with the measles, but his mother let Charlie have a wash and change his shirt before going to call for Mary Alice.

After the movie they stopped for a cherry soda at Bartlett's Drug Store. Mary Alice Flint was a farm girl, raised out on the fourth concession. She had moved into town to board at her uncle's place so that she could start high school in a couple of weeks.

They sat on the stools at the soda fountain, and Mary Alice told Charlie that she was going to be a teacher.

"I've got my future all planned out," she said. One year of normal school at the end of high school and she'd be making her own way in the world.

"I'm going to get my own little place, too, with a kitchenette and a refrigerator, and indoor plumbing." Mary Alice's uncle had the dubious distinction of owning one of the five indoor toilets in town.

"What are you going to do, Charlie?" She fluttered mascaraed eyelashes at him over her soda straw. "You're good enough to play professional baseball, you know."

"Oh, yeah, a regular Babe Ruth," said Charlie. "Only difference is I pitch right-handed." But he blushed at the compliment.

In the face of Mary Alice's high ambitions, he could hardly tell her that he was through with formal education.

At the end of the evening, when they reached the front porch at her uncle's house, Mary Alice held her face up to Charlie's expectantly. Charlie was aware that someone was standing behind the lace curtains in the living room.

"Bye, Charlie," Mary Alice said, her voice all breathy. "I had a real nice time."

Charlie leaned in close.

Suddenly, the porch light flicked on and Charlie took a step backward, stumbling down the three steps to the sidewalk. By the time he recovered his balance, Mary Alice was disappearing inside.

"I guess I'll be seeing you in school, then." She waggled her fingers at him through the crack in the doorway and was gone.

All the way back to the farm in the dark, even before he'd stopped limping, Charlie thought about her. He tried to recall every word she'd spoken that evening, and what he'd said, and whether or not it had sounded stupid.

By the time he called out to Aunt Rena that he was home and that she could go to bed, he'd determined that he would go to any lengths to see Mary Alice Flint again — even if it meant having to go to high school.

In the morning, he told his aunt that he'd changed his mind. He'd decided to take Mr. Matthie's advice and continue his education.

"I don't want you to worry about money, Aunt Rena," he said. "I should be able to work at the golf course right up till Thanksgiving, longer if it doesn't snow. And I'll try to pick up an odd job here and there.

"But if I quit school now, they say there's no steady work to be had around here. Unless you want me to go to the cotton mill, and that would mean having to pay board over in Dillfield."

Rena sliced the heel off a loaf of brown bread and handed it to Charlie. "We'll try it for a while," she agreed. "I never wanted you to sacrifice your education, Charlie. And you do have another year till you're sixteen.

"For now, though, there's a bushel of tomatoes on the back stoop. If you'll fetch it in for me, we can get started on them right after breakfast."

So it was settled — Charlie would go to high school. Of course, there still remained the problem of how he would get there, but he was confident that, sometime before the first day of school, he'd find a way.

19
Shoes for Charlie

At a ball game in early September, Delbert Coon told Charlie that Stickle's General Store was selling running shoes for twenty-five cents a pair. Seeing the sign in the window, Delbert had gone in and bought some for himself. And because Charlie had been playing ball all summer in his grandfather's old boots, he knew his friend would be interested.

"No kidding? A quarter is all?"

"Yep. Stickle's got a whole box of them," said Delbert. "I even bought two pair."

Charlie looked down at the canvas shoes his friend was wearing. Even on Delbert's big feet the shoes looked pretty flashy, and Charlie just happened to have a quarter. If he could buy a pair of running shoes like that, he'd be sure to impress Mary Alice.

Why, his feet would burn around those bases so fast they'd be smokin'.

The next day Charlie walked in to Larkin and straight to Stickle's store. He'd been here before with Mr. Fennell to buy feed, and this was where he'd bought Aunt Rena a glass pickle dish last Christmas. Besides feed and flour, dishes and glassware, Stickle's General Store carried gasoline and oil, paint and wallpaper, boots, shoes, and a few basic groceries. But not so many as to put Coon's out of business.

After sorting through the entire box of running shoes at the back of the store, Charlie discovered that all the twenty-five-cent pairs were too big.

"What about a coupla extra pairs of socks?" Mr. Stickle suggested, and he dangled a pair with red heels and toes. "Ten cents for the two of them."

"All's I've got is a quarter," Charlie said. "Anyway, I've got to be able to play ball. I'd be falling all over the place in shoes this big."

Mr. Stickle snapped his suspenders and walked away. "Can't help you then. Oh, hang on a minute. The salesman told me, in case I sold out, that he was leaving another box of these in town. No idea what size they might be."

"At another store?" Charlie was hopeful.

"At his mother's place, I believe. Over on Arthur

Road, Number 54. You know the street next to the tracks? The salesman had this funny looking wagon. Never seen anything like it, like a circus wagon. You see a big grey horse and that wagon, you'll know you've got the right place."

Charlie dropped the running shoe into the box and pulled on his old boot again.

Mr. Stickle watched him tie the frayed laces. "You know, I hate to see a man down on his luck," he said. "So I said I'd take this box of shoes off his hands."

Charlie stood up and began edging toward the door.

"He should've known better than to take a horse and wagon out on the road, selling anything," Mr. Stickle said. "Them days are over. But I guess you really can't fault a man for trying to make a few dollars, can you? Now, you take my friend Melvin ..."

The door opened to let another customer in, and Charlie slipped out.

He walked the length of Arthur Road, following the railroad tracks as far as the switch where the short line went through the fence to the canning factory. Then he retraced his steps. There was no sign of a wagon anywhere.

Number 54. He stood out front of the skinny grey house with the picket fence, frowning. He remembered this place. This was where he'd come last spring to clean out the henhouse for the lady. And Aunt Rena had made him go all the way back to the riverbank to retrieve the box of soda biscuits he'd forgotten there.

A girl was sitting on the porch in a rocking chair. She was bent over something in her lap, the pencil she held moving furiously. A small, bluish-grey cat perched on the railing. Charlie hadn't seen any girl here last spring when he'd shovelled chicken manure.

"Are you wanting eggs?" The girl's voice startled him. Charlie hadn't realized she'd noticed him.

"Naw." He shoved his hands into his pockets and rocked back onto his heels. "I heard there was a man here selling shoes."

"Not any more," the girl said. "But he took a big box of running shoes to a store downtown."

"I just came from there. They sent me here. In case you had any more of them. Those pairs at Stickle's were all too big."

The girl got up from the rocking chair, setting aside whatever she'd been doing. "Come around to the back," she said. "You can have a look in the box we put in the shed. Just go along the side of the house."

Charlie made his way to the yard behind the house and met the girl coming out the back door. He wondered if the lady was inside, watching him. She'd surely kept a suspicious eye on him the last time he was here.

The girl unlocked the door to the shed at the end of the yard. "My grandmother's over at the church," she said, as if she'd read his mind. "She helps the priest with his program for the poor."

The lady's flock of chickens occupied the other side of the shed. Charlie could hear their muffled clucking as he and the girl stepped inside.

"What size do you need?" the girl asked. She proceeded to drag a large cardboard box to the middle of the floor.

"I don't know, for sure," Charlie said.

"Well, what size are you wearing?"

He shrugged, looking down at his feet and feeling foolish. "These were my grandfather's boots. The size is all wore off."

"Oh." The girl eyed him critically. "You're pretty tall, so I'd think you probably wear a size ten. My father only wears an eight and a half."

"Ten would be about right," Charlie said, wishing she'd stop inspecting his feet. "The box at Stickle's was all elevens and twelves."

"I'm sorry," the girl said. "I guess we didn't divide them up very well."

When Charlie had found a pair of black and white running shoes that fit comfortably, he pulled a quarter out of his pocket. "Hope that's right," he said. "That's what Stickle's was charging."

"That's fine," the girl said, and she dropped the coin into the pocket of her blouse. "Whatever we get for the leftover shoes goes to my grandmother for my keep."

Charlie gave her a curious look. There was something familiar about her. Although for the life of him he couldn't remember ever meeting her before.

She had large brown eyes under thick brows and a small turned-up nose that showed her front teeth. He thought her face was kind of plain, compared to that of Mary Alice Flint, which was how he measured all female beauty these days. But he liked the way this girl had fixed her dark hair to one side, in a heavy braid that hung over her shoulder.

She followed Charlie back between the houses to the front again. He was wearing the new running shoes, his old boots tied together by their laces and slung over his shoulder.

"I hope you like them," the girl said, sounding as if she meant it. She retrieved the cat from the porch railing. "My father and I travelled all through the countryside this summer, selling shoes. We had lots of interesting things happen. I'm writing about one of them right now. I write all the time."

Charlie strolled out to the street. For the first time he noticed, below the sign that advertised eggs for sale, a second sign tacked to the fence post. "You have a horse for sale?"

The girl came to the gate, stroking the cat. "That's right. I want to keep her, but Grandmother says we can't." She cast a glance back at the house. "As you can see, there's no room here for a horse. Her name is Dora, and she's over at our neighbours' right now. Sometimes I can see her from the back bedroom upstairs."

"Well, is she for sale, or not?"

"Yes, I'm afraid she is. Papa couldn't keep her in the city, and when the man with the bread truck offered to tow the caravan back there, Papa left Dora here for us. Wasn't that kind of the bread man? He didn't even know my father. People are like that sometimes. Absolute angels.

"Anyway, Grandmother said, 'Where am I supposed to keep an animal that big at this place, let alone feed her?' Our neighbours, the Jenkins, are true angels because they are letting her stay at their place for a while."

"Can she be rode, do you think?"

"Oh, yes. She's very gentle. She's not a young horse, by any means. I was with her all summer. I love her dearly, so I'm very particular about who buys her."

Charlie couldn't help himself. "You sure do talk funny," he said.

"I do?" The girl looked puzzled. "I just speak the King's English."

"Where you from, then?"

"Toronto," the girl said, enunciating all three syllables.

Charlie nodded, figuring that likely explained everything. "I need a way to get to high school this year," he said. "So far, I've been walking in from the farm. But I might come back later, to see about that horse."

PART THREE

Home

20
News at Last

Ivy Chalmers took it as a good sign that her letter to Johnny Dracup, the Toronto baker, did not come back stamped "unknown" or "not at this address." But no reply came, either.

Weeks passed, and she started school in Larkin. Every day she waited for news of her mother's whereabouts.

Maud Chalmers had discovered, to her chagrin, that she'd missed Ivy over the summer while she was away with Alva. The girl had proved to be a bright little thing to have around, even if she was a bit peculiar.

Over the months that followed the girl's return, as she watched Ivy struggle to understand what could have happened to cause her mother to stay away so long, Maud's harsh attitude toward her granddaughter gradually softened. It worried her to see the change in Ivy, to see how the cheerful, talkative child had become the withdrawn, quiet young woman who lived with her now.

Ivy did everything Maud asked of her and more, but she'd lost her spark. Even after she started school she seemed to have no friends, other than her cat. She spent all her spare time lost in the books she got from the library. Or, now that the weather had turned cold, up in her room writing, hunched over the old washstand she used as a desk. It just wasn't normal, in Maud's opinion.

If Maud could get her hands on that self-centred Frannie, she'd shake some sense into her.

She had disapproved of her daughter-in-law from the first time she'd laid eyes on her, when she and Alva had come out here from Toronto in a motor car with a friend. Alva must have thought, because he'd neglected to do so after his first wedding, that his mother should meet the bride.

She could tell even then that Frannie had stars in her eyes and feathers for brains. Why, that woman had knocked poor Alva off his feet. And him still getting over that farm girl he'd married — the one with the ready-made family, the one that up and died on him so fast. That one was supposed to have been from around here somewhere, too.

Maud Chalmers was a firm believer in the old adage that you reaped what you sowed. One day, wherever she was, Frannie would be sorry for walking out on her only child.

⚖

Ivy finally learned the name of the boy who was buying her father's horse, on the day that he came to Maud's with a small down payment.

She remembered this Charlie Bayliss. When she'd sold him the running shoes, she'd recognized him at once. He was the boy she and Gloria had seen collecting golf balls along the Larkin road last June. But he obviously did not remember her.

Maud agreed to sell Charlie the horse and to accept his method of payment. She couldn't expect the neighbours to keep the animal all winter. She sent Ivy with the boy to the Jenkins's place to fetch her.

After Charlie had led the horse out of the gate and down the street, holding her bridle loosely and letting Dora set the pace, Ivy raced home to the upstairs window, where she watched the pair till they were out of sight. Her throat hurt as if she'd just swallowed a stone.

After that, Charlie Bayliss would appear at Maud's front door from time to time with another dollar to put toward his debt. And on each occasion, as Maud grew to trust him, he was invited a little farther into the house.

❧

Early in the afternoon of New Year's Day, 1932, the priest from St. Basil's-on-the-Corner made his careful way between the snowbanks along Arthur Road to the house where Maud and her granddaughter lived.

He'd waited all morning for the dump truck and the team of men with shovels to clear the road in front of the rectory. After yesterday's heavy snowfall, it was a relief to see the sun shine so brightly, even though the temperature overnight had plummeted.

Ivy, who was standing on a chair in the front window taking down her homemade paper decorations, saw the priest coming and called out to her grandmother. "I think you're going to have some company."

"Oh, my good heavens! And this place smelling of the soup bones I'm boiling." Waving her apron in an attempt to clear the air, Maud opened the front door. "Come in, Father. Come in."

The priest entered in a cloud of freezing vapour, rubbing his hands together and stamping the snow off his galoshes.

Maud invited him through to the kitchen where the teakettle was already on to boil.

"I'm afraid I can't stay, Mrs. Chalmers," he said. "I had a telephone call earlier this morning, and I need to have a word with your granddaughter."

Ivy flung the paper chain onto the settee and met him in the hall.

With Ivy hanging onto every word, the priest told them that a Miss Gloria Klein had called long distance, hoping that Maud Chalmers would turn out to be one of his parishioners. When he assured the caller that she was, indeed, Miss Klein had explained that she wanted to talk to Ivy and would call again at three that afternoon.

"She has some news of your mother, child," he said.

At last! Ivy clutched her hands to her pounding heart. "Is she all right?"

"I only talked with Miss Klein, so I couldn't say. She had called the Presbyterian church in town first, and she was relieved when she found out that I knew you. That's all I can tell you.

"Now, I'll be on my way, Mrs. Chalmers. Such a blessing to have a granddaughter. An answer to your prayers, I am sure."

"Thank you, Father," said Maud. "It was good of you to come all this way in the cold. Mind those steps out there. I'll have Ivy sprinkle some ashes on them."

Clutching the railing, the priest descended the stairs. "Three o'clock then," he said.

Ivy had no idea what kind of news Gloria would have for her, and she felt almost sick with worry. She was grateful that her grandmother offered to go with her to the priest's house.

Bundled in coats and scarves, the two made the trip as quickly as Maud's bunions would allow. The air was so cold that the snow squeaked under their feet.

After relieving them of their coats and galoshes in the rectory's vestibule, the priest's elderly housekeeper showed them into a small parlour. They sat and listened to the hollow ticking of the clock until, several long minutes later, the telephone rang.

Ivy leapt to her feet at the sound, hardly able to contain her excitement. The housekeeper reappeared, tottering along the hall to answer it, and only then summoning Ivy.

"Gloria!" Ivy pressed the receiver to her ear and stood close to the mouthpiece. "Is everything all right? You've heard from Momma?"

"Everything's fine, Ivy." Gloria's warm voice was reassuring. "How are you, dear?"

"I'm all right. But tell me about Momma. Is she back home? I got only one letter from her, ages and ages ago. And it was mailed right here in Ontario. I've been so afraid that she might be sick."

"She has been sick, but she's getting better now."

"Are you sure?"

"Cross my heart," said Gloria. "Frannie's here with me."

"Oh, let me talk to her!"

"I don't mean here, right now," Gloria said. "I'm calling from the bake shop. Frannie's living with me, at my place."

"How long has she been there?"

"Ever since she got back from New York."

"So, she *was* in New York."

There was a slight hesitation on the other end of the line. "Of course. You knew that." Gloria sounded puzzled by Ivy's statement.

"Gloria, you know how Momma is. Always pretending? I thought she might be making believe that she was there."

Gloria sighed. "She wasn't pretending about New York, Ivy. She had a pretty hard time there."

"A hard time?"

"She told me it all happened very fast, Ivy. That man, the director, dumped her almost as soon as she got there. Never mind all the promises he'd made. Frannie says New York City is full of girls trying to get noticed. And there she was, with no job and no money."

"So she came home."

"Not right away. She lived with a couple of other actresses for a while, and she tried to find work. She was lucky to land a cleaning job. But before she got started, she heard of a ride back to Canada. Naturally, she jumped at it.

"By the time she found out that the ride was only going as far as Syracuse, it was too late. So that's where she ended up. Eventually, she somehow managed to borrow enough money to get back across the border. And then she showed up at my place."

Ivy turned away from the mouthpiece on the wall to send Maud, who was waiting in the doorway, a look of relief. "I'm so thankful you're her friend, Gloria," she said.

"Frannie knew your grandmother would be taking good care of you," Gloria continued, "but she wanted to let you know she was thinking of you. So she wrote that letter from my place, to say everything was fine. She didn't want you to worry. That's why she told you she was still in New York City. She'll tell you the whole story when she sees you."

"When will that be?"

"I'm not sure. It would be best if you stayed with your grandmother for now. Frannie still needs to straighten a few things out before you come back."

"But doesn't she want to see me?"

"Of course she does, Ivy. But she wrote you, pretending to still be in New York, to give herself a little more time."

"More time away from me. I don't understand."

"There are things she wants to do, Ivy. You just have to be patient. You're better off where you are now. Believe me."

"Oh, Gloria!"

"Listen to me, Ivy. Half this city's out of work. You should see the lineups for the soup kitchens — all the way round the block. You can't go five yards down the street without someone asking for a handout."

Gloria continued. "My neighbour, Billy Cuthbert, who used to work in construction — you remember, you met him in the hall that time? He hasn't had work in nearly two years. They even came and took his wife's furniture, 'cos he couldn't pay for it. Now he's peddling shoelaces and pencils downtown."

"It's like that everywhere, Gloria," Ivy said. "My father, after he left here — you didn't know he was here, did you? And that I went travelling with him?

"After we got back, Papa got on a train going west, because he heard there was work out there. We got a letter from him at Christmas. He'd found a job delivering handbills. Oh, I have so many things to tell

Momma. I have to see her."

"You will; I promise. Just give her a while to get back on her feet."

"Will you ask her to write to me? Please, Gloria? What's the number on your building? I tried writing to you last summer but my letter came back."

"I won't be there after the end of the month, anyway," Gloria said. "I'm moving."

"You are?"

"I'm getting married, Ivy. You remember Johnny Dracup, at the bake shop? Of course you do. You wrote to him. He showed me your letter just the other day. That's when I decided to try to phone you."

"You're marrying Johnny?" Ivy was incredulous. "But what about Momma? Where will she go?"

"Well, Johnny and I won't put her out in the cold," Gloria said, and she gave a little laugh. "You can be sure of that. Anyway, we think in another few weeks she'll have her strength back."

"And then she'll let me come home?"

"Try to be patient with her, Ivy."

"You keep saying that. It's been an awfully long time — more than half a year."

"Try to understand."

"She is sick, isn't she? I could come and help look after her."

"She's not sick, not in the way you're thinking. She's just worn out."

"Does she know you're talking to me today?"

"I'm going to tell her; it'll help put her mind at rest. But she still has dreams of acting, Ivy. And you know better than anyone what that means. I'm telling you it would be best if you stayed where you are. Best for everyone."

◆◆

In August, on Ivy's fourteenth birthday, a card arrived from Alva. He'd tucked a wrinkled two-dollar bill into the envelope, along with a letter to say that he was back in Ontario again. He'd lost the delivery job to someone who was willing to work for even less than what he was being paid.

"Look, Grandmother," Ivy said with pride. "This is Papa's own handwriting."

"Things were no better in the west," Alva wrote, with the help of his friend John, someone he'd met on the road.

"Now we live at a camp run by the Gov't of Canada. We are cutting down trees for a new road. It is hard work for twenty cents a day. It is good to be busy. They give us work clothes to wear and three meals a day. I

181

read when I can, mostly papers we pass around. You would be proud of me."

"That was a real good thing you did, Ivy," Maud said, "helping your father with his learning."

It had been no surprise to her that Ivy, who had attended school however sporadically in Toronto, was found to be ahead of the other students her age at the stone school in the village. She finished both Junior and Senior Fourth in one year, passed her entrance exams, and was ready to enter high school in September, 1932 — just one year behind Charlie Bayliss.

21

The Typing Class

It seemed to Ivy that Charlie Bayliss had the same gentle way of handling Dora as Alva had. Much as she wished she could have kept the horse, Ivy knew that she couldn't have found a better owner for her if she'd picked him out herself.

Once she started high school, Ivy often saw Dora bringing Charlie in to school from the farm. She wasn't the only girl who enjoyed watching the pair each morning as they trotted by on their way to the drive-shed at the end of the lane. But she was likely the only one admiring the horse.

There would always be two or three girls waiting for Charlie to stride back across the yard. They'd link arms with him and come laughing into the school together.

Mary Alice Flint, the girl with the lingering summer kisses, had long been gone from Charlie's life, choosing to attach herself to Lewis Parker instead — likely because Parker's father let the boy use the family car on weekends. But it didn't take long for Charlie to discover that when you're sixteen, there's no shortage of Mary Alice Flints in the world.

Dora was of more use to Charlie than merely a means to get about more quickly. When the well on the farm went dry that summer, Charlie and his horse were kept busy hauling water from the lake.

The drought that year had reduced the quantity of milk that Edwin Fennell sent to the cheese factory each week, and that meant less money in his pocket to pay Charlie. The poor yield of hay and grain caused the farmer to worry about how he would feed the stock over the winter months, and Mr. Fennell began to sell off his herd.

It took Charlie more than a year to pay off his debt to Maud Chalmers. He made the final payment with what he'd earned picking apples on brisk October mornings before he and Dora left for school.

Ivy was fifteen and in Second Form at high school when she handed in an English assignment that she'd written — a short story about a Toronto child who had pinned all his hopes on getting a *Star* Santa Claus box at Christmastime. The dramatic twist in the tale came when the child's family was evicted from their rooming house before the box could be delivered.

The story so impressed the English teacher that Miss Derek read it out loud to the rest of the class.

"This is the best piece of fiction I've ever had from a student." The teacher had struggled to keep the tremor from her voice while she read Ivy's story. "And I've been here for a very long time."

Ivy appreciated the fact that Miss Derek told no one who had written the piece, but when she asked that Ivy stay after school for a few minutes, the secret was out.

Ivy avoided meeting the curious stares of the others as they left the classroom by focusing all her attention on scraping out the bottom of her inkwell with her pen nib.

"You write very well, Ivy," Miss Derek said, when they were alone and Ivy stood in front of the teacher's desk. "Has anyone ever told you that?"

"No, Miss. But I get a lot of practice. I've been writing my whole life."

"I think you have a special gift for it, Ivy. In fact, I'd like to see you submit this story for publication. I have *Maclean's* magazine in mind. They publish several fiction stories in each issue, and yours is as good as many I've read there."

"But it isn't really fiction," Ivy said.

Miss Derek had suspected as much. "It could be, though. You've obviously made sufficient changes to the truth."

The teacher leaned back in her chair, tenting her fingers and studying the slender girl — the white blouse tucked into a plain brown skirt, the ankle socks and sensible oxfords. She knew her to be a quiet student — one who seemed to keep too much to herself.

"You live with your grandmother, don't you? I don't suppose she has a typewriter."

"No, Miss."

"We'll have to keep an eye out, then, for a secondhand machine. Manuscripts should be typewritten before they are submitted for publication."

"Even a secondhand typewriter would be expensive, wouldn't it?"

"Come with me." The teacher was already on her feet. "I have an idea. Let's go upstairs to the commercial room, see if Miss Johnson will let you use one of the school's typewriters."

The typing teacher agreed that Miss Derek's promising young writer could have the use of a typewriter during the noon hour and after school. But since Ivy was going to have to prepare future manuscripts herself, Miss Johnson suggested that she really should learn to type properly.

After studying various schedules and seating plans, the teachers determined that there was room for Ivy in a Third Form typing class. The class, except for two students, was made up entirely of girls. The two exceptions were Delbert Coon and Charlie Bayliss.

Delbert was taking an office-training course because his father felt it would come in handy when he joined the family business. Charlie was there because Delbert had talked him into it — and because the only other choice was Latin.

"It's a real good way to meet girls," Delbert had promised. "The class will be full of them; all the peachiest girls want to be secretaries, you know. Anyway, typing's a breeze."

But both boys realized how wrong that was when they discovered, on the very first day, that the typewriter keys were blank.

When Ivy entered the classroom for the first time, she found that the space Miss Johnson had assigned her was at a machine directly in front of Charlie's. She made her way as quickly as possible toward her seat, eyes lowered, sidestepping the other girls, who wandered around exchanging gossip.

Charlie sat with his arms behind his head, his chair tilted back against the wall. He was more or less listening to Irene Noyes, who had perched herself on the edge of his desk. But at the same time, he was keeping an eye on the rest of the room.

The minute Miss Johnson strode in, everyone scurried to take her seat. Irene hopped blithely off Charlie's desk, colliding with Ivy and sending her books flying.

Charlie was on his feet in an instant, crouching down to help collect the scattered books, coming face-to-face with the girl from whom he'd bought the horse.

His smile widened. "Didn't expect to see you here," he said.

Ivy felt the heat rise in her face. She took her books from him, mumbled an embarrassed "thank you," and slid into her seat.

It was bad enough being the new girl in a class of older students, a class that was already halfway through the term, but to have created such a commotion on her first day, and in front of Charlie Bayliss, too, made her want to crawl into a hole.

When the class was over and everyone was leaving, Irene sidled up to Charlie again. She gave Ivy a frosty glare. "So, who's your little friend, Charlie?" she asked.

Before he allowed Irene to lead him like a puppy from the classroom, Charlie managed a wink at Ivy.

Later, Charlie found himself thinking about Irene's question. He knew very little about this girl named Ivy Chalmers, except that she lived with her grandmother, and that she had spent a summer with her father, selling shoes from the back of a peddling wagon.

Now he was sorry, with the horse fully paid for, that he had no further excuse to call at the house on Arthur Road. Ivy Chalmers interested him, in a curious sort of way. She was not like any other girl he'd ever met.

Ivy was still on Charlie's mind a few days later when he happened to spot her leaving the school. Telling Linda Darling that he'd have to see her later, he galloped down the steps and arrived on the sidewalk before Ivy did.

"Hi, Ivy Chalmers," he said.

"Hi, yourself," said Ivy. She hoped she didn't look as surprised as she felt.

Charlie fell into step beside her and was suddenly unable to think of anything to say. He cast an incredulous eye at the pile of books she hugged against her chest. "What form are you in that you have so much homework all the time?" was what he came up with.

"It's not all the time," Ivy said. She wondered how he would know about the number of books she took home every night — unless he'd been watching her. "I just like to keep up. And to answer your question, I'm in Second Form."

"But you're in Third Form typing."

"It's the only Third Form class I'm in. And I take it because I plan to be a writer."

"Oh, that's right. You do it all the time. A writer," Charlie said. And then he said it again, as if he were trying out a new word.

He was still walking with her when she turned off the main street onto Arthur Road. They moved to either side of a group of little girls playing hopscotch on the sidewalk, and when they had passed them, Charlie said, "I never met a writer before."

"I haven't either," said Ivy. "I've read lots of different ones, though."

"Anyone else in your family a writer?"

"Well, you've met my grandmother. And my father has done lots of different things, even gold mining in Northern Ontario."

"No kidding? What about your mother? Is she a writer?"

He seemed to be teasing now. "She's an actress," Ivy stated.

"In the movies? Say, I saw *Frankenstein*, with Boris Karloff, at the Roxy last week. You see it?"

"I'm afraid not."

"So, what's your mother's name? Maybe I've seen her in the movies sometime."

"You haven't. My mother is a stage actress. Her name is Frances Chalmers. But her friends all call her Frannie."

"Is she famous?"

"I'm not sure. I know she'd like to be." Ivy hesitated. She stole a cautious look at Charlie's face, longing to tell him — this boy she felt connected to in ways she could not fully explain.

She shifted the weight of the schoolbooks onto her hip. When Charlie offered to carry them for her, she politely declined and walked on.

"My mother went to New York, and everything," Ivy found herself confessing. "She was going to be a star. The director promised her the lead in a new play, but then he broke his promise. I think that was so mean. She had to come back to Toronto. I'm just waiting to hear if things are better, and then I'll go home, too."

"You're going back to live in the city?"

"One day. I only came here to stay with my grand-mother till my mother made a name for herself. But that was more than two years ago."

They'd reached the picket fence at the front of Maud's place. Soon she would go inside and he would lose her.

Ivy paused a moment, her hand on the gate, remembering something. When she turned toward Charlie again, she was wearing a frown. "Where's Dora?" she asked.

Charlie's jaw dropped. He'd completely forgotten about the horse. "She's back at the school," he said, with a gulp.

Ivy fiddled with the latch on the gate, hiding a smile, knowing then that Charlie must have walked this way on purpose, just to be with her. "I was afraid something might have happened to her," she said.

"Oh, no. She's real fine." Charlie spoke quickly to cover his embarrassment. "I've been meaning to tell you. The farmer next door, Mr. Fennell, has a couple of horses, and when he lets them into the field next to our place, you should hear Dora. She whinnies like crazy. She really likes their company."

"That's good to hear," said Ivy. Giving Charlie a smile, she slipped through the gate.

Growing Up Ivy

Charlie waited till the green front door had closed behind her. When it had, he ran all the way back to school, periodically giving little leaps into the air.

22
Literary Friends

When Harry Pike saw Charlie wheel through the gates of the Shady Dell Golf Course on a bicycle, and learned that the youth had restored the bike himself, he made a mental note to mention the boy's ability to his brother-in-law, who owned the repair shop in the village.

Edwin Fennell had given Charlie the old bicycle as payment for helping him fill his woodhouse before winter. Charlie had been happy to accept it. He'd never before owned a bike.

He tinkered with it on and off for weeks, removing its chain to clean and oil it, scraping away the rust on the frame, straightening and tightening the spokes, and patching a hole in one of the tires.

Charlie was pleased with the final result. The satisfaction he'd felt working on the simple machine led him to take a second look at his grandfather's collection of old tools that had been gathering dust in the shed. After sorting and cleaning them, he began to look for excuses around the farm to put them to use. Rena could always find something that needed fixing.

When the snow finally melted, Charlie rode his bicycle to the Larkin District High School and was able to give Dora the rest she deserved.

❧❧

Maud Chalmers had gradually increased the size of her flock of laying hens, knowing she could count on Ivy's help with their care and feeding, and with the gathering and washing of the eggs. And Ivy had had to accept that a two-year-old hen that no longer laid eggs could provide a Sunday dinner for someone — as long as it wasn't her.

Early one Saturday morning in the spring, as Ivy was helping her grandmother carry the eggs to the market, she spotted her English teacher choosing stalks of fresh asparagus at the next stall.

"There's Miss Derek," Ivy said. "She's the one who said I was a good writer."

Maud had been outraged that *Maclean's* magazine had rejected Ivy's story. She had not the faintest idea what the story had been about, nor how good it was, but she held Miss Derek responsible for heaping more disappointment onto Ivy's plate.

"I feel like giving that woman a piece of my mind." Maud jammed eggs into an empty carton. "She had no business putting such big ideas in your head."

"Please don't say anything," Ivy pleaded. "I guess writers have to get used to having their work rejected. I'll just write something else and try again."

Miss Derek had already expressed her own disappointment at hearing that the manuscript had been returned. "Maybe we aimed a little too high to start with. But it was a good experience for you, dear, even if not a happy one. We'll take a look at some smaller markets next time."

❧

If Ruth Vernon hadn't approached Ivy about joining the school's Literary Committee she would never have considered going to one of their meetings, even though Miss Derek had told her the committee had chosen a short essay that Ivy had written and one of her poems for the yearbook.

Ruth had been in the same class as Ivy since starting high school two years before, but neither girl had spoken more than a dozen words to each other.

Ivy was surprised to find Ruth waiting for her outside the classroom one day. "Ivy, can you hold on a minute?"

"Of course."

"The others on the Literary Committee wanted me to ask you if you'd like to come see what we do, at our next meeting."

The others? Could that mean that insignificant Ivy Chalmers had crossed the mind of more than one person? It cheered her to think so.

"There are ten of us on the committee," Ruth explained. "Elections aren't till the fall, but we have lots to do before school's out for the summer. We'd like it if you'd think about joining us. You're such a good writer, Ivy."

"I think I'd like to come," Ivy said, warmed by the sincerity in Ruth's tone.

"Okey dokey, then. We're meeting in Miss Derek's room at noon hour tomorrow. Can you bring your lunch? I notice you usually go home at noon."

❧❧

Ivy nearly backed out when she saw the number of people in the English room at lunchtime the following day.

"It's not always like this," Ruth said, drawing Ivy through the doorway. Excited chatter filled the air, and everyone seemed to be in a great hurry, rushing back and forth.

"The Yearbook Committee's here, too, and they're ready to do the final layout. The two committees sort of overlap this time of year.

"Those kids over there — you'll recognize them — they're the ones who took all the class photos for the book. That bunch at the front ran all over Larkin, begging local merchants to buy space for a small advertisement.

"Come on, I'll introduce you to Opal Forbes. She's helped me with all the mimeographing."

Opal Forbes, Ivy discovered, also happened to be in her Third Form typing class. With her almost-white hair and translucent skin, Ivy felt the girl's name suited her well.

"Once the yearbook's done, things will settle down," Ruth promised. "Then, when we get together at meetings, we can work on our own writing. Sometimes one or two of the kids will want to share their work with the group."

"But you don't have to," Opal said quickly. "Some people are a little shy about that. And we always talk about the books we've read; that's the best part of our meetings. I've seen you at the library, Ivy. Have you read *Wild Geese* by Martha Ostenso yet? You haven't? Oh, you have to!"

Miss Derek slipped in to check on progress, and by the time one o'clock rolled around, Ruth had managed to introduce Ivy to everyone in the room. Those who could stop cutting and pasting long enough shook her hand or called out "hi," as if she were already part of the team.

Until that day, Ivy had no inkling that there were others in the school who shared her interests. Or if there were, how to find them. Thanks to Ruth, she'd found a place in a special community of friends. Suddenly, the whole world looked brighter.

23

Jiggs

Charlie's work for Edwin Fennell, who only six years earlier had bought most of the Bayliss farm, came to an abrupt end in June 1934, when the man was felled by a massive heart attack.

Charlie and Aunt Rena were wakened early that morning by the bawling of Mr. Fennell's half-dozen milk cows, protesting their full udders. When Rena appeared at his bedroom door, long hair falling loose down her back, Charlie was already buttoning his pants. "I'm on my way," he said.

The dog, Jiggs, did not come to meet him as she usually did, and when the farmer wasn't in the barn, which Charlie had come to expect at that hour, he sprinted to the house.

He found the man sitting in the armchair he kept

in the kitchen, looking as if he'd just sat down to rest a spell. His supper plate lay smashed on the floor at his feet, the food on it untouched, even by the dog.

Nineteen thirty-three had been the worst year yet for the area's farmers. But Edwin Fennell would never have to struggle through another.

Mr. Fennell's married daughter, Jean, came to stay in her father's house until arrangements could be made to put the farm up for sale. On the day of the funeral, Jean had one final request to make of Charlie.

"I want you to choose one or two of Dad's things that you would like to have for yourself, Charlie." She gripped the youth's hands as they stood in the parlour of the little house, too close to the coffin for Charlie's comfort. "A keepsake or two. I don't care what."

Charlie fixed his gaze above the heads of the mourners, on the view of sky beyond the open door. "Well, I don't really know," he said.

"Anything," Jean said. "Dad appreciated all you did for him. I'm sure the pay couldn't have been much, at least not lately. He told me how you like to fix things, Charlie — some of his tools, perhaps?"

"Thanks, but I have my Grandpa's tools." Charlie brought his eyes down to meet hers then and was suddenly touched by her kindness. "I'll have a look around," he said.

"Just promise me you'll choose something. And don't wait too long, Charlie, or there'll be nothing left."

Mr. Fennell's daughter stayed long enough to see her father's cattle go for five dollars a head at auction. After she'd gone, Charlie realized that she'd made no arrangements for Jiggs's care. The farmer's black and white border collie had been Charlie's constant companion while he did his chores at the farm. Now he wondered what would become of her.

"Maybe whoever buys the house will take her," Aunt Rena said, as she scraped cold porridge into a pan for the dog's breakfast. "I'll see that she's fed till then."

"Or maybe," Charlie said, "we could just keep her ourselves." But every evening, in spite of Charlie's urging, the dog insisted on returning home to curl up on its own doorstep for the night.

On the day that Charlie was supposed to be with his friends at the Larkin District High School's annual end-of-year picnic, he and the dog were driving Edwin Fennell's small flock of sheep to their new home, down past the crossroads.

The successful bidder for the sheep was impressed by the way Jiggs single-handedly moved the animals along the road, through the gate, and into the paddock. "That's a smart dog you got there," he said. "She part of the deal?"

"Nobody said she was." Charlie leaned his arms on the gate beside the farmer's to watch Jiggs's performance for a minute. "Those there are her sheep, though."

The farmer scratched his chin. "Well, I don't want to put her out of a job. I'll take her, if she'll stay."

Charlie had not intended to leave the dog behind, but she was focused on herding the sheep into the pen, circling the flock in that low crouch of hers, defying any stragglers. If a sheep tried to break away, Jiggs would lie down, lower her head, and fix the animal with her characteristic gaze. It worked every time.

Charlie swallowed hard. "Her name's Jiggs," he said and turned quickly away.

Walking back home, he tried to tell himself that it was only natural for the dog to want to stay with the flock. Letting her go was the kindest thing he could do for such a well-trained animal. Best to try to forget about her.

He was on the far side of the crossroads when he heard the sound of heavy panting and flying feet behind him. He turned to see Jiggs racing toward him, her tongue hanging out the side of her mouth.

Charlie caught the breathless dog up in his arms and carried her the rest of the way back. She had made her choice, he thought, and it was to go home with him.

He opened the door of the house just long enough to call out, "We've got ourselves a dog!" and then hurried over to wash under the backyard pump. There might still be time to get to the school picnic.

Someone hailed him as he was crossing the yard to fetch his bike. He looked over to see a beat-up '27 Chevy truck pulled into the yard next door.

"We're here to pick up the goods we bought at the auction." The driver was squeezing out from behind the wheel.

"I'll get you the house key," Charlie said.

A big woman in a faded housedress came around the truck. "And could you give us a hand with it? Frank here has a bad back and shouldn't be lifting nothing."

Charlie Bayliss had never been farther than the two front rooms of the little house himself. Mr. Fennell had done most of his living right there in the kitchen, often sleeping on the narrow cot next to the cookstove.

The second Charlie opened the front door, Jiggs burst into the house. Her nails clacked frantically on the wooden floors as she raced from room to room and up the stairs, searching for her master.

Charlie had not forgotten his promise to Mr. Fennell's daughter, and now he cast his eyes around the two upstairs rooms. One room appeared to have been set up as the farm office, with a wooden swivel chair and an oak desk. But Aunt Rena had told him that she already had more than enough furniture.

After unloading papers and boxes from the top of the desk, it took three people to manoeuvre it and a mirrored wardrobe down the narrow stairway and out to the truck.

By the time Charlie made it to the fairgrounds where the school picnic was being held, it was late afternoon. All the students had left. The few teachers that had remained behind were rolling up the oilcloth from the tables and finishing off the cake.

Mr. Stevens, the history teacher, watched Charlie turn around and ride back out through the gates. He wondered out loud how many female hearts the youth had broken that day by his absence.

"I find he's a likeable lad," Miss Johnson added. "One can't blame him for his good looks."

And Mr. Stevens, a skeletal man whose nose came close to meeting his chin, knew that to be the truth.

With nothing else to do, Charlie biked on out to the Pechart River, sure that he would find Delbert Coon and some of the other boys there at the tail end of a hot day.

Delbert failed to notice him till Charlie had swung out over the deep hole and dropped off the end of the rope, landing in the water beside his friend.

"Where the heck were you?" Delbert demanded, when Charlie shot to the surface, flipping the hair back out of his eyes. "You missed the whole darn thing."

"I was at Mr. Fennell's. Couldn't get away."

He turned then and, with smooth strokes, swam out beyond the group and let the current pull him downriver. Then he swam back, enjoying the feeling of strength in his arms as they drew the water toward him.

"Hey, Charlie," someone called. "Darling Linda was looking for you at the picnic."

"And you know that girl in the typing class?" Delbert asked.

Charlie righted himself, treading water. "Which one?"

"That Ivy girl."

"What about her?"

"Nothing," Delbert said, floating on his back. "I was just sort of surprised that she showed up."

"She come with anyone?" Charlie tried to sound nonchalant.

"Couldn't say. I didn't see her come in. Saw her talking to that bunch that worked on the yearbook. I don't remember seeing her again."

Before it was time to go home, Delbert and Charlie clambered up the riverbank to relax with the other boys. With school out, the talk naturally turned to plans for the summer ahead.

The Classon twins were leaving in the morning to go to work on a farm over near Dillfield. "Slave labour," they called it, remembering last summer — long hours with few rewards, except a roof over their heads and the leftovers from the farmer's table. But it meant two less mouths for the family back home to feed.

One by one the group of youths broke up and headed home for supper, until Delbert and Charlie were the only ones left. After this summer they wouldn't see much of each other. Delbert would be leaving for Belleville in September, where he would board with an aunt and attend Ontario Business College. Charlie was waiting to hear whether or not Harry Pike's brother-in-law would take him on at his repair shop. He considered himself fortunate to have kept his weekend caddying job. Unless one could find an odd job here or there, there was nothing else.

Suddenly, Delbert gave his forehead a slap. "Oh, no! I was supposed to ask the guys if anyone wanted to pick strawberries for the store. Ma's going to kill me."

Charlie wriggled back into his shirt. "Why don't you pick 'em yourself?"

"She's got me painting shelves," Delbert said. "I'm not even halfway done. Besides, it's hot as blazes at Elders' strawberry field."

"I'll take the job," Charlie said. "I'm done at Fennell's now. Tell your ma I'll do it."

"Sure thing," Delbert said. "You got any of those baskets left?"

Charlie shook his head. He'd been collecting six-quart baskets wherever he could find them because Coon's Grocery paid a cent a piece for them. "Not since I took those in last week."

"Come on down to the store," Delbert said. He picked up his bike. "I'll get you enough to get started."

With the baskets strung along his handlebars, Charlie decided to take the long way home. He cycled back through the town and over to Arthur Road, just on the off chance that he might see Ivy.

24
One Penny at a Time

Just as Charlie had hoped, Ivy was sitting on the front porch, pencil in hand, her cat curled around her feet.

"I hear you were at the picnic today," he called out.

Ivy raised her head, suddenly aware that the sight of him made her pulse quicken. "I was," she said. "I didn't see you, though."

Stretching long legs out on either side of the bike, Charlie folded his arms across his chest. "I was finishing up at Fennell's," he explained. "Since Mr. Fennell died, there's been a lot to do. His farm's up for sale now."

When Ivy bent to lift the cat into her lap, he said, "Got myself a dog now, too. She was Mr. Fennell's, but I've been feeding her since he passed on, so I think she's mine. Her name's Jiggs."

"Dogs are nice," Ivy said.

"Say, what happened to your gate?" Charlie asked, noticing that it was propped against the fence.

"The screw nails fell out again."

Maud Chalmers had had someone repair the gate twice already since spring, but it refused to stay that way. It was one of several odd jobs around the place that she had found for the men who came by looking for work.

These transients, some of them painfully young, rode into town on the freight trains and walked the streets, hoping to find employment. But there was nothing here. The town of Larkin couldn't afford to pay even its own out-of-work citizens the relief money they might have been entitled to in a larger city.

The men reminded Maud of Alva, and although she couldn't afford to pay cash for the little jobs they did, she always fixed them a hot meal and let them sit on her back stoop to eat it.

Charlie lowered the bike to the ground and came to assess the problem of the broken gate. "It just needs some longer screw nails," he said. "I could come by and fix it for you." It would be another excuse to see her.

After an awkward silence, he asked, because he was not yet ready to leave, "What are you writing now?"

"I think it's a short story," Ivy said, pleased at his interest. "I might send it away to a magazine if I think it's any good when it's finished. It has to be typed first, though. Grandmother and I are saving up to buy a secondhand typewriter. But it's one penny at a time."

"I know how you can earn a little extra money," Charlie said, "if you're interested."

"How's that?" She left the porch and walked out to where Charlie stood.

"Picking strawberries for Coon's Grocery Store."

"Really? I wondered what the baskets were for."

"I'm starting tomorrow. Mrs. Coon will take all we can pick. So, you want a job?"

"I do," Ivy said. "I'll run in right now and tell my grandmother."

When she returned she was carrying a basket of her own. "Grandmother wants me to see if they'll trade some berries for eggs."

"I'll pick you up tomorrow on the bike, then. Seven-thirty? Best to get there before it gets too hot."

"I'm sure I can walk. Grandmother said she used to walk out there herself, before her feet got so bad."

"Suit yourself," Charlie said, "but it's likely two miles, at least."

Early the next morning, Ivy joined the procession of pickers carrying pails and baskets and picnic lunches along the road to Elders' berry farm. Whatever the job, there were always more than enough workers to fill it.

Charlie, coming from the opposite direction, met her about halfway. He'd rigged a wooden crate to the back fender of his bike and filled it with empty fruit baskets. Ivy declined his invitation to ride the rest of the way on the handlebars.

She quickly discovered that picking strawberries was hot work, and she was glad she'd rolled up her long hair and tied it with a scarf. In spite of the heat and having to bend over the low plants to find the fruit hanging underneath, the berries were the size of small plums, and it didn't take long for Ivy and Charlie to fill all their baskets.

After dropping off Maud's berries and telling her that Elders would take a dozen eggs in exchange, they delivered the rest to Mrs. Coon and collected their pay for the morning's work.

Charlie had brought with him a pocketful of assorted screws to repair the gate at the Chalmers's place.

"It's only temporary," he said, when Maud came out to inspect the job.

"Seems it is, every time it gets fixed," said Maud.

"That's 'cos the wood where the hinges are attached is rotten and should be replaced," said Charlie. "I'll see if I can find some pieces at home that would do the trick."

Ivy's grandmother went into the house and returned with a glass of water for him. When Charlie saw that she had put some ice chips in it, he felt as if he'd passed some sort of test.

On Friday, Charlie told Ivy that he had to work his regular job at the golf course the next day and would not be going berry picking. Unfortunately, it was going to be the last weekend for the strawberries. They were getting smaller and harder to find due to the lack of rain, and the Elders wanted to use their own pickers for the last of the crop.

Ivy went out to the berry farm herself on Saturday, chatting with some of the other women as they moved slowly down the rows. She stayed just until she'd picked what she could carry back herself.

"We'll be opening again in a couple of weeks for the raspberries," Mr. Elder explained as Ivy counted out what she owed him. "Come back then, but be sure to wear long sleeves. The canes are real prickly."

Ivy told him that she would be back. After today, she was two dollars closer to that typewriter.

❧

Harry Pike had some good news for Charlie when he met his young caddy at the golf course that Saturday.

"Floyd says to come round the repair shop when you can, son, and you can talk to him about helping him out. There likely won't be much in the way of money, but you can learn the ropes, see if it's what you want to do."

"That's good enough for me," Charlie said.

While dropping off the berries to Mrs. Coon yesterday, he'd learned that in September he could take over for Delbert, delivering groceries on his bike. The six dollars a week the job paid would suffice until the repair shop could afford to pay him a wage.

The round of golf over, Charlie lifted Mr. Pike's bag of clubs into the car for him. A gust of wind caught the newspaper the man had left on the seat, sending it out into the parking lot. Charlie scurried after it, scooping up pages and trying to put it all back together again.

"Take it if you want it," Mr. Pike said, with a wave of his hand. "That paper's a week old. I want to drive with the windows down anyway, and it'll just blow all over the place."

Charlie forgot the paper in his bike carrier when he got home, and it wasn't until Sunday morning that he noticed it there. He brought it inside to give to his aunt.

Rena Bayliss hadn't spared the nickel it took to buy a newspaper in some time. She immediately spread the

Mail & Empire out on the dining room table and sat down to read.

She was still there an hour later when Charlie came into the room and began rummaging through the drawers in the sideboard, looking for a pencil to mark the measurements on the pieces of wood he needed for the gate at Maud Chalmers's place.

"That's odd." Rena leaned closer to the paper in front of her. "I wonder if it can be the same person."

"Who can?" asked Charlie, jamming a finger into his mouth. He'd speared it on an old pincushion that had been hidden in the drawer.

"This person in a play over at Port Clear — Frances Chalmers."

Charlie wasn't listening.

"That's exactly the same name as that girl your father married — after your mother died."

"My stepfather, you mean." Charlie shoved everything back into the drawer and pushed it shut. "His last name was Chalmers? I never knew that."

Rena nodded, without looking up. "Did I never mention it? Well, it's not important. He wasn't in our lives for long. I just met him the one time, after Dottie's funeral."

She turned to the next page. "Lots of people have the same last name. It's likely not her at all. Your stepfather called her Frannie or something, and that's usually short for Frances."

Rena refolded the newspaper and set it behind her on the sideboard. "Enough time wasted for now," she said, getting to her feet. "I've got that old sweater to unravel. Knit us up some good, warm socks."

Before Rena was even out of the room, Charlie snatched up the paper and scoured its pages till he found what his aunt had been reading.

It was an advertisement: Frances Chalmers, starring as Norah, the lead role in a play called *A Doll's House*. She was part of a touring summer theatre troupe currently performing in Port Clear.

Because he'd never been aware of his stepfather's family name until now, Ivy's name had not rung any bells for him. But he did know, because Ivy had told him, that her mother was a stage actress named Frances Chalmers.

Could this actress, now appearing in Port Clear, be the woman Ivy had been waiting for, for so long? And more important to him, could Ivy's mother and the woman his stepfather had married after his own mother died, be the same person? Or was that just too much of a coincidence?

Charlie sat back against the chair. That would mean that his stepfather was Ivy Chalmers's father, the shoe peddler. Holy smoke! He and Ivy could be some sort of distant relatives!

Charlie tore the ad from the paper and slipped it into the pocket of his shirt. Then he went back to the barn and began sawing the boards for Maud Chalmers's gate.

❧

Maud put an end to Charlie's theory of connectivity with her usual lack of grace. "Practically family? Nonsense! You two are not related in any sense of the word."

She'd known that Alva had brought Dottie's child back to its grandparents, where it belonged, after the young woman's untimely death. But how was she to know that child would turn out to be young Charlie Bayliss?

"I always thought Alva told me Dottie's name was Bailey," she said, in her own defence.

And who would have guessed that Charlie would start coming around here, on the flimsiest of excuses, to see Alva's girl, Ivy?

Now, sitting in her rocking chair on the porch, watching how deftly Charlie trimmed away the punky wood and fitted the new sections into the gate, she found that she rather liked the idea of having him as her step-grandson.

Ivy, crouched on the front steps, had read the advertisement until she could recite it from memory, and with each reading, the level of her anxiety grew. There was no doubt in her mind that this was Frannie. Ibsen's play, *A Doll's House*, had been one of her mother's favourites.

But the paper that had printed the ad was already a week old. Frannie's play would end its Port Clear run this Sunday.

"I remember the strangest dream I had that summer I spent with Papa," Ivy said. "In my dream I was looking everywhere for Momma, but then she came and told me not to try to find her. I wasn't even looking for her then."

Maud pleated the apron on her lap with nervous fingers. "Could be some folks don't want to be found."

"But I've got to try, Grandmother. You know that I do. It was just a silly dream. I have to go to her, now that I know where she is."

Port Clear wasn't that far away, and Ivy could get there by bus. She'd use her strawberry money to pay for her ticket. Forget the secondhand typewriter, this was her mother — and so close at hand.

"I can't lose her again. She'll only be there till the

end of the week. Who knows where she'll go after that?"

Maud realized that there would be no stopping her, but she was equally sure that the girl was headed for another disappointment. She told Charlie as much, while the two of them were searching the shelves in the back shed for a bit of paint to touch up the new wood on the gate.

"You know, I'll be eighteen next month," Charlie said. "I could go with her, if you'd feel better about it. That is, if Ivy agrees."

In the end, that was the only way Maud would allow it.

25

Finding Frances Chalmers

Charlie cycled into Larkin on Thursday morning, well ahead of the bus's scheduled departure for Port Clear. He had a stop to make before he met Ivy, and he didn't want to risk her seeing what it was that he carried in the crate on the back of his bike.

When Charlie came through the door of Floyd's Repair Shop, the owner looked up from the toaster he was rewiring. "Mr. Bayliss," the man said, "I thought I asked you to come in next week."

"You did, sir. But I have something I'd like you to take a look at." Charlie set a rigid black case on the counter, right under the man's nose.

Floyd Hutchins, possessed of the same need as Charlie to know how things worked, set aside his pliers. Releasing the catch on the case, he lifted the lid to reveal a small typewriter, its carriage folded down over the keys.

When Charlie had first seen it on the desk in Mr. Fennell's upstairs office, he had paid little attention to the case with Corona 3 stamped on the lid. It was only when he got thinking about what it was that Ivy was saving her pennies for that he remembered the case, and went back to see if it was still there. He found it still sitting on the swivel chair, where the couple who'd bought the desk had set it.

Suddenly, he knew that this was what he would accept from Mr. Fennell's personal belongings.

"Hope you didn't go putting oil on this." Floyd Hutchins, fingers down in amongst the type bars, looked over the top of his spectacles at Charlie. "'Cos if you did, I'm going to have one heck of a time unclogging it."

"I didn't," Charlie said. "I know someone who really needs this typewriter, so I didn't want to mess with it. I thought I'd better have you check it over."

"Nice little machine," Hutchins said, after a few seconds' further inspection. "Very handy how the front of that case folds out. You can use the machine while it's still inside.

"That bit of string there, see it? It goes from the main spring to the carriage, and it's broken. That's your problem."

Floyd Hutchins pushed his spectacles up over his bushy eyebrows and turned his gaze on the lanky youth on the other side of the counter. "This is something you could do yourself, Mr. Bayliss — you've got those long fingers.

"If there's nothing else I need you to do when you come in next week, you could work on this. I'll tell you everything you need to know. Then, with a little cleaning and dusting, it'll be ready for your friend."

He closed the case and slid the typewriter onto the shelf behind him, returning his attention to the toaster.

Charlie wandered around the shop for a few minutes, looking at the worktable filled with manuals, the tools and equipment for repairing radios, and the various items awaiting the repairman.

"You familiar with radios, Mr. Bayliss?" Hutchins saw Charlie pick up one of the vacuum tubes and examine it closely.

"No, sir," Charlie said. "We've never had electricity on the farm. My friend Delbert has a radio, though. I've listened to the programs at his place. I sure would like to know how it works."

"There's a lot more to it than *Amos 'n' Andy*," Floyd Hutchins said. "Anything else, Mr. Bayliss?"

"I guess not. I'm just trying to get an idea of the kinds of jobs you do here. Hope to have my own repair business one day."

"Better wait till there's enough work to keep us both alive," Hutchins said.

⋘⋙

Ivy and Charlie were the only ones waiting for the noon bus at the gas station in town that day. Charlie drew lines in the dirt with the side of his shoe and hoped he'd be able to keep his secret about the typewriter until it was ready to present to her.

Ivy paced, playing with the clasp on her purse, surprised at how nervous she was. She'd been preparing for this reunion with her mother for three years, yet now that it was at hand, she found that her stomach was queasy, as if she were about to give a recitation in front of a roomful of strangers.

The bus to Port Clear and points west was almost full, but Ivy and Charlie found seats kitty-corner across the aisle from each other.

Ivy noticed that Charlie kept rubbing his hands on the knees of his baggy grey trousers and glancing back at her. *What reason did he have to be anxious?* she thought.

With the announcement that the next stop would

be Hardyville, the woman sitting beside Ivy stood up to retrieve her bags from the overhead rack. Ivy slid over next to the window.

The bus stopped to let the woman off, and Charlie came to sit with her. "You all right?" he asked, aware of the grip she had on the purse in her lap and of her rigid posture.

Ivy grimaced. "I guess so." She wished she could relax. "I keep asking myself why — if my mother is well enough to go back on stage — she didn't at least write to me. She's been in Port Clear for two weeks. It really does look as if she plans on going home without getting in touch with me. Does she intend to leave me with my grandmother forever?"

"Would that be so terrible?"

"It would be nice to know, one way or the other."

"Well, you'll have all the answers soon," Charlie said. "And if it makes you feel so bad, try not to think about it. We could talk about something else."

"Like what?"

"How about your father? You could tell me just about anything about him and I'd believe you. All's I know for sure is that he was kind to my mother and me. And Aunt Rena said that after he got married again he came out to see me one time. But I didn't remember him and he never visited us again."

"That's too bad," said Ivy. "Let me see now. Yes, Papa's kind. And he's generous, too. You know, Charlie, he'd have given you that pair of running shoes for free, if he thought you really needed them."

She was thoughtful for a moment. "If you met my father you'd find he doesn't say much. You might think he's shy, but he's not. You should have seen him when those people in Birch Hills confronted us.

"Sometimes I felt that Papa had this air of sadness about him. I think it's because of the life he's had. He's the kind of man that keeps a lot of things to himself, anyway. Maybe he never met anyone who was interested in hearing what was on his mind."

"Until you came along," Charlie said. "Next time he comes to visit you, I'd sure like to meet him. Properly, this time."

"You're going to be one big surprise, Charlie Bayliss," Ivy said, smiling. The tension in her shoulders had eased; the change of subject had helped.

Opening the bag lunch that Maud had packed for them, she handed Charlie one of the hard-boiled eggs. She unwrapped an oatmeal cookie for herself, but when it was still lying in her lap, untouched, as the bus pulled in to Port Clear, Charlie offered to eat it for her.

They stepped off the bus in the centre of a small town that hugged the shore of a picturesque bay.

Sunlight danced on the water. A banner, strung across the main street, announced a summer festival of plays and band concerts.

The Port Clear Theatre was a peeling clapboard building next to the town dock. It reminded them both of Willards' Dance Hall back in Larkin. The back half of the weathered structure stood on tall piers in the water, allowing boaters to tie up underneath. A side door opened onto the wharf and an adjacent park with a bandshell.

Neither Ivy nor Charlie had tickets for Frannie's play, nor did they have enough money to buy them. But Ivy was not worried. She had no doubt that she would get into the theatre to see her mother. The name "Frances Chalmers" would be the password that opened the doors for her.

The two stood in front of the theatre and studied the schedule of performances tacked behind the glass of the display case. There was a one o'clock matinee and an evening show at seven. Since the matinee had started a half-hour ago, they would wait till the final curtain and catch up with Frannie when she left the theatre.

"It says that *A Doll's House* is a three-act play," Ivy said. "They likely have an intermission before the last act. The actors might even step outside for a bit of air, and if they do, they'll probably use that door on the side."

With no other choice but to wait for that to happen, they wandered into the park and sat down on a bench where they could keep an eye on both the front and side doors.

Charlie ate the last of the lunch and then strolled, by himself, along the main street, returning to tell Ivy that there was a café across the road where they could buy a cold drink or a hot dog.

"You go," Ivy said. "I'll stay here and keep watch."

As soon as the front door of the theatre opened, signalling the end of the matinee, Ivy hurried from the park to get a closer look at the people exiting the building.

The audience had been a small one. A handful of people drifted up the street or crossed to the café, and one couple boarded one of the rowboats moored at the wharf. There was no sign of Frannie or anyone else that Ivy thought might have been part of the cast.

Within five minutes, a man whose moon face shone with perspiration came out onto the sidewalk. He looked both ways up the street, stepped back into the theatre, and pulled the door shut.

Ivy immediately knocked on the door.

The man opened it just enough to stick his head out. "Next show's at seven. Box office opens at six."

"Please." Ivy got her fingers around the edge of the door. "My mother is the star of the show. Frances

Chalmers? I'd like to speak to her."

"Sorry. The cast gets a few hours to rest now, between performances. You can see her after the final show."

"But I'm her daughter. I've come on the bus, and I want her to know that I'm here."

"Sorry. There'll be time for the public to meet the cast later."

"But I'm not the public!"

The man yanked the door out of her grasp and shut it firmly. Ivy heard the scrape of the lock on the other side.

Charlie sauntered across the street. "No luck?"

Ivy was indignant. "That's absolutely ridiculous! How am I going to let her know I'm here? I can hardly believe all that's separating me from my mother is a couple of walls."

"If this was the Roxy, back home," Charlie said, "I'd get you in for the next show."

"Without a ticket?"

"Someone inside would have to agree to prop that side door open."

"And who would do that?"

Charlie grinned and shrugged helplessly. "That's the way we used to sneak into the movies when we were kids. We'd pool our money and buy one ticket between us. Then, the kid with the ticket would go in and sit down, and when no one was looking, he'd shove a stick in the side door to keep it open, just a crack.

"After the movie started and the theatre was dark, the rest of us would sneak in through the side door and sit in the front row, all scrunched down so the usher couldn't see us."

"I'll bet that usher knew you were there all the time," Ivy said. "It's an old trick. Come on. I've got a much better idea."

Charlie followed her back into the park where she dropped onto the nearest bench and pulled a notebook out of her purse. Tearing a sheet of paper from it, Ivy scribbled a few lines to Frannie.

Momma,

I read in the paper that you were here, and I've come on the bus from Larkin. I can't believe we're this close, but I'm not being allowed inside. The man at the door says I can't talk to you until after the last show. But the bus leaves at 10. I am waiting right outside.

Love,
*   Ivy*

A slightly larger crowd began to gather outside the theatre for the evening performance. Ivy joined the lineup at six o'clock. Just inside the door, a freckled youth, wearing a red bowtie, sat behind a table with a hand-printed sign that read BOX OFFICE.

"One ticket?"

"I'm not buying a ticket," Ivy said. She spoke slowly and clearly, so that there would be no misunderstanding. "I want to let one of the actresses know that I'm here. Frances Chalmers. I'm her daughter."

"If you haven't got a ticket, you can't go in," the ticket seller said.

"I know that. All I want is for someone to hand this note to Frances Chalmers."

"You can't go backstage."

"But you could, couldn't you? Or you could give it to someone to put in her dressing room."

With a heavy sigh and an aggrieved look at the people waiting behind her in line, the young man took Ivy's note and slid it under his cash box. "Next!"

"It's very important," Ivy said, before she turned away.

She stepped out of line and walked back outside to take up her vigil again. How long would it be before Frannie read her note? When she had, would she come to the door and look for her?

At seven o'clock, the same round-faced man who had argued with Ivy earlier came and shut the front doors.

Charlie showed up again to check on her. "We could go back into the park," he suggested. "Unless you want to wait in the café."

"I'm going to wait right here," Ivy said. "Now that she knows that I am this close, she may call me to come inside."

But that didn't happen. Before the performance was over, Ivy had counted all the nails in every board on the front wall of the Port Clear Theatre and traced each crack in the sidewalk a dozen times.

As soon as the front doors were thrown wide to let the audience trickle out, Ivy strode in. No one stopped her this time.

She made her way through a maze of loose chairs on the auditorium floor to a door beside the stage. A few members of the audience were waiting there for the cast to emerge.

Ivy opened the door and marched through, closing it behind her.

26

Return to Larkin

There were two doors off the hall that ran along the back of the stage to the side exit of the Port Clear Theatre.

Inside the first, Ivy found a dingy washroom with dripping fixtures. The other door opened into a large room that was being used as a dressing room by the actors. By squeezing through a rack of costumes that had been pulled across the doorway, Ivy managed to get inside. The room was noisy and crowded, the air thick with cigarette smoke.

Frannie stood with her back to Ivy, applying cold cream to her face from a large jar. Ivy was aware of the exact instant in which her mother saw her in the mirror.

Frannie whirled around. "Ivy! My sweet, sweet girl! It really *is* you! Oh, no. Don't hug me yet." She seized a towel off the dressing table. "You don't want greasepaint on your blouse."

Her face sufficiently wiped clean of makeup, Frannie turned from the mirror, clasping her hands to her breast. "What a wonderful surprise! I can't believe it's you.

"But you really shouldn't have given me such a shock, Ivy. Once I knew you were here, I could barely get through the last act, and it's such a dramatic one, too — when Norah makes her decision. You remember, don't you? Finally standing up for herself?"

"I remember," Ivy said. "Momma, let me look at you. Oh, you look so well. When Gloria said you'd been sick, I expected you'd be all skinny and pale. But you look wonderful."

Frannie ran her hands down over the silky slip that draped her slim figure. "Do you really think so? It's not always easy ..."

"I've waited so long to hear from you, Momma."

"Let me get dressed, dear heart, will you? Then I'll come out and we'll talk our little heads off." Plucking at some clothing that hung over a folding screen, Frannie disappeared behind it.

"I'll be out in the hall, then," Ivy said, afraid of going too far away.

Already it seemed as if there was something missing from this reunion. But it was early, and Ivy tried to dismiss the feeling of disappointment building inside her.

A few minutes later, Frannie emerged, wearing a cotton sundress. She threaded her arm through Ivy's as if they were best girlfriends, and they left the theatre together, through the side door. But just on the other side, they were accosted by a handful of people, eager to have a word with the star of the show.

Ivy lingered at the edge of the conversation for a while, growing increasingly impatient. Time was slipping away.

At last she managed to catch Frannie's eye, and her mother made an announcement to her fans. "I'm afraid I really must leave you all now. This is a very special night for me. My daughter, Ivy Rose, has come a long way to see me, and I must have some time with her. You all understand, don't you?"

Amid murmurs of protest, Frannie walked away, trailing a hand. "No, I really can't. Good night now, everyone, and thank you for coming."

They made their exit.

Charlie, who had been leaning against the front

of the café across the street, straightened up and watched them come toward him. Ivy was the taller of the two. The older one — the mother — was a looker, all right, but she lacked Ivy's high colour. He hesitated before deciding to follow them into the café.

There was an empty booth near the back, and Charlie stood aside to let the women have their choice of seats.

"Sit across from me, Ivy dear," Frannie said, "So that I can feast my eyes on you. There, that's better."

Without a word, Charlie slid in next to Ivy, and she gave him a bleak smile. It made him fear that things were not going as well as she had hoped.

"Now, tell me. Did you see the show?" Frannie's voice was breathless, her clear, blue eyes wide.

"No, we didn't. Momma …"

"Oh, shame on you! You really should have. It's quite wonderful. It got very good reviews when we played in Brockville. It ran a full three weeks there. Next week we go to Orillia."

"But how could I have known where you were, Momma? It's been so long since I heard from you. A lot has happened. Gloria said she would ask you to write to me."

"It *has* been a long time." Frannie sat back in the booth, studying her daughter. "You're almost sixteen, aren't you? And, my dear, you have turned into quite a beauty."

"Oh, Momma, I hardly ..."

"Yes, you have."

Frannie's gaze fell on Charlie then, for the first time acknowledging his presence. "Isn't she a little beauty? Well, not little, exactly; but you know what I mean. She always was tall for her age."

Charlie mumbled something and Ivy felt embarrassed for both of them.

Knitting her finely drawn eyebrows into a frown, Frannie examined the youth. "Who is this handsome young man, Ivy? Is he your beau, then?"

"No, he's not my beau, Mother. This is Charlie Bayliss, a friend of mine."

"M-m-m. Very handsome indeed. Or is that red hair of yours a curse?"

"Mother, please! Charlie was kind enough to come with me today because Grandmother didn't think I should come alone."

"Pleased to meet you, ma'am," said Charlie, and he extended his hand across the table.

Frannie held it longer than was necessary, putting her other hand over it and batting her eyelashes at him. Ivy had forgotten this mannerism of Frannie's, and now she found it irritating.

"You want to know who he really is, Mother?" she demanded. "He's my father's stepson. Did Papa ever tell you he had a stepson?"

Frannie's smile got even brighter, and she showed no surprise whatsoever at the announcement. "Yes, I remember. Alva's first wife already had a little boy. Just a baby, I think. And that's you, Charlie? How exciting! Where are you living now?"

"I live where I've pretty near always lived. With my Aunt Rena, outside of Larkin."

"That year you left for New York, Mother," Ivy said, "I spent that whole summer with my father. Did Gloria tell you that he found me? He came to Grandmother's before he went travelling, and we finally got to meet each other. I asked if I could go with him, and he let me.

"We had a wonderful time getting to know each other. After that, he went out west for a while. But he's back in Ontario now. He writes me letters sometimes. Did you know he's learning to read and write? And he sends money to Grandmother whenever he can."

No one spoke while Frannie absorbed this rush of information. Charlie cleared his throat uncomfortably and climbed out of the booth. "I'm going to watch for the bus, Ivy," he said. "I'll let you know when I see it."

The clock above the soda fountain said 9:45.

"Oh, Momma," Ivy said. "I'm sorry about all that. We haven't got much time. Why didn't you tell me you were back in Toronto? We could have been together. When were you going to tell me?"

Frannie smoothed an invisible tablecloth in front of her and looked at her hands. "It was supposed to be a surprise for you, Ivy. I'm sorry Gloria went and spoiled it. I was waiting till my situation was a little better." She met her daughter's eyes again. "But I'll be sending for you soon."

"How soon?"

"When this touring company gets back to the city. In a few weeks. Audiences are a little thin this year — we may have to close ahead of schedule. I think I'll try to find a regular job when I get home."

"That means you're going to give up acting?"

"Well, no. I'll never be able to give it up altogether. I may still do a little, on the side. You know what they say — once the theatre is in one's blood ..." Her voice trailed off.

"Oh, Ivy darling, don't look so disappointed. When I'm settled, we'll get a place and be together again. Like old times; just you and me. I remember how it was. We were a real team, weren't we? Can't you just *make believe* that we're together? You used to have such a wonderful imagination."

"I still have a good imagination," Ivy said. "I need it for the stories I write. I've already had some of my fiction published at school, Mother. But this is my real life — it's not make believe."

The door of the café flew open. "Bus is coming," Charlie called out. Immediately, several other customers stood up to leave.

Frannie slipped quickly out of the booth, but Ivy clutched at the sash on the back of her dress, suddenly overcome by the feeling that this might be the last time they saw each other. "Momma, listen. I don't have to go. I could stay here with you."

"Ivy, you know you can't do that."

"Why not? Where are you staying?"

"In a room at the hotel down the street. There are eight of us in two rooms."

Charlie was signalling frantically from the open door. "Come on, Ivy. They're loading up."

"Please, Momma. We could be together." Without wanting to, she had become that small child again, begging Frannie to take her with her, filled with the old fear of abandonment.

"Ivy, there are five women in the room now, and two kids."

"I'll sleep on the floor."

"You coming, Ivy?"

Ivy hurried to the door. "You have to go, Charlie. You've got to tell Grandmother that I'm staying with my mother."

"When are you coming home, then?"

"Momma's here till Sunday."

"You want me to tell her you won't be home till Sunday? She's going to be awful mad."

The waitress at the counter spoke up then. "Oh, Miss? There's no other bus after this one, till next Tuesday."

"Ivy," Frannie said. "You must go."

"I can't lose you again, Momma, now that I've finally found you."

Charlie was out on the step, gesturing at the bus driver to be patient. Instead, he sounded the horn rudely.

"If you're staying, I'm staying," Charlie said, and he stepped back inside. "I'll go tell the driver to go without us."

"No, no, you can't! That's not fair! Grandmother will be frantic if you don't go back and tell her."

Ivy cast a desperate glance over her shoulder. She caught Frannie in the act of smoothing her hair in the mirror above the lunch counter, wetting the two little kiss curls on her cheek with a finger, and running her tongue over her lips.

For an instant their eyes met.

Recovering quickly, Frannie put a hand on Ivy's shoulder and propelled her toward the door. "You said it yourself, Ivy; this is your real life. You need to be sensible now."

The bus had already started to pull away from the curb when Charlie grabbed Ivy's hand and drew her down the steps of the café. He used his other hand to wave down the driver, who brought the vehicle to a wheezing stop. When the door opened they climbed on board, ignoring the glares of the other passengers.

Charlie guided Ivy into the nearest seat and dropped down beside her. He didn't dare look at her. He expected she would be furious at him for dragging her away. It would probably be best to keep quiet until she was ready to speak, if she spoke to him again.

It was a long time before Ivy turned to face him with a wan smile. "That was awful, wasn't it?" she said. "There were so many things we needed to talk about, and I wasted time trying to find out when she was going to ask me to come home."

"Did she tell you?"

Shaking her head, Ivy replied, "No, not really. But I don't think my mother can answer that question, anyway." She let out a shuddering sigh.

"My mother hadn't laid eyes on me in three years, and she wanted to talk about her play and why we hadn't seen it. I don't know why that should surprise me. That's the way it's always been. Nothing gets in the way of Frannie's acting career. Not even me. Other people knew the truth about her already. But I didn't see it. Till now."

"Well, how could you?" Charlie said. "Weren't you just a little kid when she left?"

"I was twelve-and-a-half. I think I knew the minute I saw her in the dressing room today that she had everything she wanted."

"I'm real sorry, Ivy," Charlie said. "Maybe we shouldn't have gone."

"No. It's good that we did. Because now I know what I have to do. It's quite simple. From this day on, I'm just going to accept that Frannie will always be Frannie, and I'm not going to expect her to be any different."

Ivy turned her face to the dark window and saw her reflection there. It surprised her a little that she looked exactly the same as she had that morning. She thought that there should be some outward evidence of what had just happened to her.

She laid her head against the back of the seat, filled

with a wonderful sense of being a whole person at last, and the only one responsible for her happiness. No matter what her mother decided to do next, Frannie no longer had the power to disappoint her.

Ivy saw the look of bewilderment on Charlie's face and it made her smile. "It'll be all right, Charlie," she said. "I'm not a little kid anymore. If you come by tomorrow, you'll probably find me writing about what happened today. I'm writing my life story, you know. And today feels like another chapter."

"Am I going to be in your story?"

"Why?" Ivy asked. "Are you part of my life?"

"Maybe I'd like to be," Charlie said.

For a moment they looked into each other's eyes, until Ivy, understanding what he meant, had to look away.

Charlie gave a little laugh and broke the spell. "Aren't I already part of your family?" he asked. "I mean, sort of? On account of your father?"

He put his hand over hers where it lay between them on the seat. When she didn't immediately snatch it away, he curled his fingers around hers and kept them there all the way home.

The bus dropped them off in Larkin just before midnight. The moon had disappeared behind heavy cloud and the night was very dark. The gas station had closed. A heavy shroud of insects all but oblit-erated the light from the single bulb at the front of the building.

Charlie had arranged to stay overnight at Delbert's, where he'd left his bike, but he'd promised first to walk Ivy back to 54 Arthur Road.

The lamp was on in the living room window; Maud was waiting up for her. When Ivy opened the front door and saw her sitting there, she wondered if it might have crossed her grandmother's mind that she would not return.

She heard the soft plop of Merlin's feet as he jumped to the floor, leaving the warmth of Maud's lap to come and wind himself around her legs.

❧

One month after Ivy's sixteenth birthday, and three months after they'd last spoken, a letter arrived from Frannie.

She was still living with Gloria and Johnny (those true angels), an arrangement that would last only until she could find work. Any day now she expected to hear of an audition for another play, and she thought it would be a very good idea for Ivy to stay with her grandmother for a while longer.

Growing Up Ivy

Ivy was quick to reply, typing her letter, with only a few mistakes.

```
54 Arthur Road
Larkin, Ontario
October 3, 1934


Dear Mother,


I was very ghappy to receive your
letter last Wednesday. Please keep
writing to me and I will always
write back. If you would send me
your address, I wouldn't have to
send my letters in care of the
bakeshop.
     I have an after-school job now,
helping out in the office of the
Larkin Courier. One of my teach-
ers told me they were looking for
someone. I am mostly just tidying
up, but it makes me feel like a
real writer, just to walk through
the door. Nnow that I have my own
typewriter (one day I will tell
you that funny story), I am going
to be writing a weekly column of
school news for the Courier.
     pPromise me that you will take
care of yourself, and please do not
worry about me. Grandmother and I
```

get along fine. She says that I am
good for her. And Charlie Bayliss
has asked me to be his girl.

Your loving,
    Ivy.

Author's Note

Over the years, such books as Hugh Garner's *Cabbagetown* and Bernice Thurman Hunter's Booky series for children have fuelled my interest in the lives of everyday Canadians during the Great Depression. I was fortunate to have been born a decade after the worst of it was over, but I have always been fascinated by the stories of those who lived through it.

There was the young boy, barely into his teens, who had to quit school for a factory job in order to help support a large family, where the only other income was the dollar a day his father earned by cutting wood. There were the housewives who used to beg the butcher for bones for dogs they didn't have, because dog bones were free. In the cities, some folks scooped up manure after the delivery horse had gone down the street in order to fertilize tiny kitchen gardens. They relied on the windowsill in the wintertime to keep the milk cold; in the summer they would resort to a sink filled with cold water. Everyone had his own story of hardship of some kind.

I first learned the story of the original "Ivy" in letters she wrote to me when I was researching a book of local history. She was by that time in her eighties and living in California. Her real name was Nellie. When she was a young girl she used to spend a few weeks every summer with her father, a peddler, roaming the countryside in a horse-drawn caravan. As I read Nellie's letters I tried to imagine that unusual home-on-wheels, "all fitted out inside so's a body could live there."

It had been a hard life for the father, but his daughter had only happy memories of those barefoot summers. Her story was the inspiration behind *Growing Up Ivy*.

Selected Reading

Bonisteel, Roy. *There Was a Time*. Toronto: Doubleday Canada, 1991.

Braithwaite, Max. *The Hungry Thirties: 1930–1940. Canada's Illustrated Heritage*. Toronto: Natural Science of Canada, 1977.

Broadfoot, Barry. *Ten Lost Years, 1929–1939: Memories of the Canadians Who Survived the Depression*. Toronto: McClelland and Stewart, 1997.

Garner, Hugh. *Cabbagetown: The Classic Novel of the Depression in Canada*. Toronto: McGraw-Hill Ryerson Ltd., 1968.

Green, Bob. *Eavesdroppings: Stories from Small Towns When Sin Was Fun*. Toronto: Dundurn Press, 2006.

Heron, George. *Child of the Great Depression: Growing Up in Downtown Toronto During the 1930s.* (Self-published) Select Press, 2005.

Hunter, Bernice Thurman. *As Ever, Booky.* Richmond Hill, ON: Scholastic-TAB Publications, 1985.

Hunter, Bernice Thurman. *That Scatterbrain Booky.* Richmond Hill, ON: Scholastic-TAB Publications, 1981.

Mallory, Enid. *The Remarkable Years: Canadians Remember the Twentieth Century.* Toronto: Fitzhenry and Whiteside, 2001.

Swerdferger, Rowat. C. *The Way It Was.* Kingston, ON: Brown and Martin, 1977.

More Great Fiction for Young People

Jailbird Kid
Shirlee Smith Matheson
978-1-55488-704-0
$12.99 £7.99

Angela Wroboski has recently moved with her mother into the city to escape a dark past. Her dad, the infamous Nick "The Weasel" Wroboski, has served three jail terms for various crimes, and on June 5, Angela's fifteenth birthday, he's released from a two-year sentence. The Weasel tries to prove that this time he's going straight. But the influence of the old gang, led by notorious Uncle Al, who's now operating a "business" that's more than a little shady, remains a constant threat to Nick's future as a family man. When Angela learns that a crime is being planned that could blow apart her family, she must quickly decide how to intervene without breaking her father's code to "never discuss family business outside the home."

Wild Spirits
Rosa Jordan
978-1-55488-729-3
$12.99 £7.99

Eleven-year-old Danny Ryan and nineteen-year-old Wendy Marshall think their friendship is only about looking after two baby raccoons that Danny has rescued. But after a bank holdup, Wendy leaves her job as a teller, retreats to a farm, and surrounds herself with injured and orphaned wildlife. Danny, neglected at home and shunned by the other boys in town, finds peace on the farm, too, as he and Wendy adopt ever more exotic animals, including llamas, bobcats, and a blind lynx. Over time the two friends develop a bond that goes beyond care of the animals to caring for each other. As it turns out, Wendy rescues not just wildlife, but Danny, as well. What's more, the bank robbers are still at large and still a threat, and Danny, now fourteen, must act to save Wendy's life.

Girl on the Other Side
Deborah Kerbel
978-1-55488443-8
$12.99 £7.99

Tabby Freeman and Lora Froggett go to the same school, but they live in totally opposite worlds. Tabby is rich, pretty, and the most popular girl in her class. Lora is smart, timid, and the constant target of bullies. But despite their differences, Tabby and Lora have something in common — they're both harbouring dark secrets and a lot of pain. Although they've never been friends, a series of strange events causes their lives to crash together in ways neither could have ever imagined. And when the dust finally settles and all their secrets are forced out into the light, will the girls be saved ... or destroyed?

Available at your favourite bookseller.

DUNDURN PRESS
w w w . d u n d u r n . c o m

What did you think of this book?
Visit www.dundurn.com
for reviews, videos, updates, and more!